PENGUIN CLASSICS

CANE

JEAN TOOMER (1894–1967) was born and raised chiefly in Washington, D.C., in the household of his grandfather, P. B. S. Pinchback, the first African American to serve as governor of a state, Louisiana. A writer, educator, and spiritual seeker, Toomer blazed like a comet through the literary firmament with the appearance of *Cane* (1923), which awed and inspired African American writers of the Harlem Renaissance and later. Toomer partook of both black intellectual traditions and the leftist and avant-garde cultural radicalism of Greenwich Village. Finding his creative imagination fired by southern black folk life during a brief stint as principal of a black industrial school in northern Georgia, he wrote a series of poems, sketches, stories, and plays in the early 1920s, many of which he composed into his modernist masterpiece. He considered it a lyrical "swan song" to a form of life that would soon die in the "modern desert," while contributing essentially to the advent of a new "American" culture and people. Following *Cane*, Toomer made a spiritual journey through various psychological and religious experiments for which he was an admired proponent and teacher, until finally harboring in the Society of Friends.

ZINZI CLEMMONS was raised in Philadelphia by a South African mother and an American father. Her debut novel, *What We Lose*, earned her a spot on the 2017 National Book Award 5 Under 35 list and was a National Book Critics Circle John Leonard First Book Prize finalist. Clemmons lives in Los Angeles with her husband, where she teaches at Occidental College.

GEORGE HUTCHINSON is Newton C. Farr Professor of American Culture in the English department at Cornell University. He is the author of *The Harlem Renaissance in Black and White*; *In Search of Nella Larsen: A Biography of the Color Line*; and *Facing the Abyss: American Literature and Culture in the 1940s*. He also edited *The Cambridge Companion to the Harlem Renaissance* and co-edited *Publishing Blackness: Textual Constructions of Race since 1850*.

JEAN TOOMER

Cane

Foreword by
ZINZI CLEMMONS

Introduction by
GEORGE HUTCHINSON

PENGUIN BOOKS

PENGUIN BOOKS

An imprint of Penguin Random House LLC
375 Hudson Street
New York, New York 10014
penguinrandomhouse.com

First published in the United States of America by Boni & Liveright, Inc., 1923
Published in Penguin Books 2019

Introduction copyright © 2019 by George Hutchinson
Foreword copyright © 2019 by Zinzi Clemmons

LIBRARY OF CONGRESS CATALOGING-IN-PUBLICATION DATA
Names: Toomer, Jean, 1894–1967, author. | Clemmons, Zinzi, writer of
foreword. | Hutchinson, George, 1953– writer of introduction.
Title: Cane / Jean Toomer ; foreword by Zinzi Clemmons ;
introduction by George B. Hutchinson.
Description: New York, New York : Penguin Books, 2019. | Series: Penguin
Classics | Includes bibliographical references.
Identifiers: LCCN 2018029324 | ISBN 9780143133674 (paperback)
Subjects: LCSH: African Americans—Social life and customs—Fiction. |
African Americans—Southern States—Fiction. | Racism—United
States—Fiction. | BISAC: FICTION / African American / General. | FICTION
/ Classics. | FICTION / Literary.
Classification: LCC PS3539.O478 C3 2019 | DDC 813/.52—dc23
LC record available at https://lccn.loc.gov/2018029324

Printed in the United States of America
3 5 7 9 10 8 6 4

Set in Sabon LT Pro

Contents

CANE

Foreword

Originally published in 1923, *Cane* was written in an era not so different from ours, and Jean Toomer embodied the prevailing artistic movements of his time and context—modernism and the Harlem Renaissance—as both a writer and an individual. His literary experiments with fragmentation and hybridity placed him firmly alongside James Joyce and T. S. Eliot. At the same time, he also found fellowship among luminaries such as Alain Locke and Zora Neale Hurston, who committed themselves to dynamically representing African American experiences on the page. Though not usually acknowledged in the historical record, or given his due in the mainstream canon, Toomer deserves to be considered a respected figure in both movements.

These artistic movements occurred against the backdrop of the Great Migration, a decades-long period, beginning in the late nineteenth century, when thousands of blacks fled the agrarian South for industrialized labor in the north and west. This migration occurred—much as it is in the Middle East now—because blacks were escaping increased racialized terror resulting from state actions such as the 1896 *Plessy v. Ferguson* decision, which legalized "separate but equal," and the subsequent Jim Crow laws that brutally upheld segregation.

In light of this, Toomer also devoted much time and thought—possibly even more than his writing—to how he constructed his own identity. Toomer was of black and white heritage, and appeared racially ambiguous. New research by the scholars Rudolph P. Byrd and Henry Louis Gates Jr. suggests that he passed for white at various points in his life. In the same essay, Byrd and Gates noted, "Anticipating the curiosity, confusion, and misunderstanding that his body, speech, and appearance would engender, and no doubt seeking to escape the boundaries imposed upon persons of African descent, Toomer tells us he formed his own 'racial position' before leaving what he would have us believe was a 'special' race world of Washington, D.C."[1]

Toomer's "racial position," as described in his journals, was "an aristocracy . . . midway between the white and Negro worlds" composed of mixed-race people. This position would later inspire him to imagine a new race for himself, an extension of his actual position in Washington, D.C.—a midpoint between blacks and whites from which he could communicate with both. He called this new race "American," and it was both an invention and a foreshadowing of one of the many ways in which race is reimagined today.

Between 1929 and 1967, following initial publication in 1923, *Cane* fell out of print. Since then, editions were published in 1969, 1975, 1988, 1993, 2011, and today. In 2010, new research on Toomer was revealed. *Cane* is having another moment today, and it doesn't seem coincidental. After the failure of post-racialism and the shortcomings of the first black president (increasing inequality, the worsening economic situation of African Americans) have been aired, *Cane*'s importance has again been recognized.

In the wake of Barack Obama's election, the term *postracial* emerged to potentially characterize the moment Americans found themselves in. With the election of a black president, and the country's demographics tilting toward a majority-minority, it felt like we might have shed those old, constrictive notions of race. We had broken through a barrier, shattered a glass ceiling, and certainly none of those old prejudices could survive in this brave new world. Today, *post-racial* feels like a quaint artifact of a more hopeful time, a time we dared to imagine ourselves beyond the country's many deep-seated racial tensions and frequent outbursts of violence.

Toomer, in his work and life, is one of the truest illustrations of *post-racial*. In her essay on multiracial identity and the new American president, "Speaking in Tongues," Zadie Smith invents a homeland for post-racial, mixed-race people like Toomer, called Dream City. She describes Dream City as "a place of many voices, where the unified singular self is an illusion. Naturally, Obama was born there. So was I."

Though she arrives at this point through different means, Smith implicitly connects multiracial identity to Toomer's own "racial position." Both are middle points from which dialogue between black and white can happen—a parallel construction to Toomer's "Americans." She explains why this is true: "In Dream City everything is doubled, everything is various. You have no choice but to cross borders and speak in tongues. That's how you get from your mother to your father, from talking to one set of folks who think you're not black enough to another who figure you insufficiently white."

Smith doesn't define Dream City as post-racial, but it is clear that this is the space popular culture was attempting to find post-2008 but never could. Barack Obama—because of his racial position, she implies—came close. But Dream City never actually existed in real life—except, perhaps, in that genius slogan from the Obama campaign, "Yes We Can!"

This special place was only ever tangible in the imaginations of its would-be citizens.

I first discovered *Cane* when I think many black intellectuals do—in college. There was an unmistakable atmosphere, a buzz, that accompanied this book. My fellow classmates and professors spoke about it in hallowed terms. For black intellectuals and academics, we who find inordinate pleasures in obscure objects, this was a hidden gem, a treasure. *Cane*'s obscurity lent to its legend. This was a book too unusual for high school, its author too controversial and contradictory for your typical college class. This was a book that was approached only by the avant-garde and questioning, its format too confusing for the average reader; its pages would only yield to the open-minded. In short, it was a well-kept secret.

Nevertheless, *Cane* feels not so obscure now, but it has not lost its magic. The early aughts, when I was an undergraduate, were a particularly poor moment for representation of people like me. We held works of art like *Cane* against the commercialized images of blackness we were used to seeing stand in for us, our thoughts, our artwork. No, in the past few years, *Cane* has become increasingly relevant. It even feels, now, retrofitted to this precise historical moment.

At the turn of the century, roughly when Toomer wrote *Cane*, the world was experiencing rapid advances in technology, politics, philosophy, and art. The United States went through a Great Depression and then, in close succession, two world wars. In the past twenty years, we have seen the largest recession since 1929, escalating conflict in the Middle East, and a resulting refugee crisis whose effects have been felt, in one way or another, in most countries on earth. The internet and social media have drastically changed how we interact, consume media, shop, and even date. New powers are emerging, which means that new ethnic conflict will not be far behind.

Toomer, like the other residents of Dream City, like those who foolishly thought the post-racial moment had arrived, was punished for his imagination. Jean Toomer never wrote another book after *Cane*; he was too busy chasing the ghost of his identity. His moment never arrived, until perhaps today. *Cane* is not a perfect book. It doesn't provide solutions. I'm unsure there are solutions to what problems ail us today. But that was never the point of this book. *Cane* gestures toward the heavens, allows us to look beyond what lies before us here on earth. We may not have achieved a post-racial America, but *Cane* encourages us to look beyond what is in front of us, to imagine a world beyond the one we live in today.

ZINZI CLEMMONS

Introduction

Jean Toomer's *Cane* was greeted in 1923 by influential critics as the brilliant beginning of a literary career. Presenting
an unprecedented perspective on the South generally and on
black southerners in particular, it inspired African American
writers and would-be writers, pointing the way forward—
away from shame about the past and present of black southern folk culture, toward pride in the beauty of blackness.
Many stressed the "authenticity" of Toomer's African Americans and the lyrical voice with which he conjured them into
being. His treatment of black characters contrasted starkly
with both the stereotypes of earlier work by (mostly) white
authors and the then-current limitations of African American problem fiction. As Montgomery Gregory pointed out in
the new black magazine *Opportunity*, Toomer had avoided
"the pitfalls of propaganda and moralizing on the one hand
and the snares of a false and hollow race pride on the other
hand."[1] Many agreed with the novelist and critic Waldo
Frank's statement in the foreword to the book: "It is a harbinger of the South's literary maturity: of its emergence from
the obsession put upon its mind by the unending racial
crisis—an obsession from which writers have made their indirect escape through sentimentalism, exoticism, polemic,

'problem' fiction, and moral melodrama. It marks the dawn of direct and unafraid creation."[2]

Key to the unusual features and effectiveness of *Cane* was the fact that its author was in rapid transition, vocationally, geographically, socially, and intellectually, between different identities. His unsettled position derived from both a complicated personal history and the unusual cultural moment and places in which he emerged as an artist. *Cane* exemplifies how the texts that do most to renovate literary traditions are often subversive of the very notion of tradition; their authors are not so much unitary figures inhabiting fixed cultural coordinates as people who straddle the threshold of social differences.

Born just two years after his famous grandfather, P. B. S. Pinchback—a former governor of Louisiana during Reconstruction—had moved from a palatial home in New Orleans to a smaller, though fashionable, house in Washington, D.C., Toomer never really knew the father for whom he was originally named.[3] His mother, Nina, gave birth to him just nine months after a wedding of which her father disapproved, and then found herself abandoned when Nathan Pinchback Toomer (as Jean was first named) was only a year old. Nina moved back to her autocratic father's home, on condition that she change the boy's surname to Pinchback and his first name to anything other than Nathan (her husband's name). Eventually, the first name became Eugene, after a godfather, but friends called the boy "Pinchy." His mother called him Eugene Toomer; his grandparents, Eugene Pinchback. Ambiguity of identity and a strong intuition of the arbitrary nature of social labels came early to Toomer.

He would later represent the social world of his youth as peculiarly unmarked by racial consciousness, but he attended a "colored" primary school on U Street while his white friends attended a different school. After his mother's 1906 remarriage, a move to a white neighborhood in New Rochelle on Long Island Sound, and then his mother's death in 1909, Eugene returned at age fourteen with neither father nor mother to the Pinchback family in Washington, where his grandparents now lived in his uncle Bismarck's home on Florida Avenue, in a mostly black neighborhood. He would later remember this milieu as one of a genuine distinction in culture, manners, and learning. Yet his family belonged to Washington's "colored aristocracy," a group that considered itself above most black people in manners and education. After graduating in 1910 from the famous, all-black M Street (later Dunbar) High School, he began consciously to think of himself as neither black nor white—or both black and white, belonging to both worlds and yet, because of that, removed from each. Because of his famous family, his friends considered him a Negro, but he decided to simply let people take him for what they wished while he maintained a sense of being outside their clumsy categories.

Toomer entered an agricultural program at the University of Wisconsin—where he was apparently taken by many for a Native American—but dropped out after only a year. His interest in modern scientific agriculture and agricultural technology, joined with what he later learned from Marxist sources, informs his notion of the transformation of the rural South that pervades *Cane*. The "cane" of the book is that of sorghum, a plant brought from Africa during the slave trade. Throughout the southeastern United States, the cane stalks of sorghum were crushed for their sap, which was then boiled to make molasses, the chief sweetener in southern homes. Sorghum molasses, moreover, was a key ingredient for moonshine whiskey in the early twentieth century. Yet in the 1920s and 1930s it was being replaced by cane sugar as new roads integrated the southern countryside into larger national and international economic networks, networks that helped carry moonshine north via "bootleggers in silken shirts," to quote from the opening of the second section of Toomer's book.

In January 1916 Toomer entered the American College of Physical Education in Chicago. Fellow student Meridel Le Sueur, later a famous left-wing poet, would remember Toomer as "reserved, isolated, perceived as an Indian by the rest of the students."[4] A boxing instructor introduced him to socialism, and he began attending lectures by the famous left-wing lawyer Clarence Darrow and others on naturalism, atheism, and social radicalism. These overturned his prior notions of the world, and he began seeking a comprehensive theory of contemporary reality. He enrolled at the University of Chicago but dropped out after only a few months. Returning east, he took a sociology course at New York University's summer school, then studied history at City College while he stayed with his uncle Walter. World War I broke out and he went back to Chicago, where he sold Ford automobiles and began writing while reading Bernard Shaw. Then he took a short-term job as a substitute physical education director in Milwaukee. The story "Bona and Paul," the first of the pieces that would later make up *Cane*, may well have been drafted at this time.

After returning to Washington with neither a job nor a vocational plan, Toomer once again moved to New York to take a clerk's post with a grocery firm. He attended lectures at the left-wing Rand School of Social Science and there met radical writers associated with journals such as *The Liberator* and the *New York Call*—the first to which he would soon begin submitting his work. Marxism profoundly impressed him with its comprehensive theory of history, which he melded with his developing theory of race in American life, and which partly underlies the sociohistorical vision of *Cane*.

About the same time, influenced by Romain Rolland's novel *Jean-Christophe* (which featured a composer-prophet fusing German and French spiritual inheritances into pan-European music), he decided to become a composer and took a second job as a physical education director in a settlement house to pay for music lessons and piano rental. He adopted the name Jean, inspired by Rolland's hero and Victor Hugo's Jean Valjean. He attended more lectures by socialists and cultural radicals; read Ibsen, Santayana, and Goethe; bummed around upstate New York during the summer of 1919; and placed two pieces with the socialist *Call*—his first appearance in print.

In his later autobiographical manuscripts, Toomer played down the extent of his interest in socialism. His two pieces for the *Call*, a voice of the Socialist Party of America, clearly reveal, however, that he had found in Marxist theory a compelling framework for understanding racial as well as class exploitation. The socialist strain remains evident in references within *Cane* to "powerful underground races" threatening the foundation of bourgeois Washington. In a letter to his publisher while *Cane* was in press, Toomer described a new book project about "this whole black and brown world heaving upward against, here and there mixing with the white. The mixture, however, is insufficient to absorb the heaving, hence it but accelerates and fires it. This upward heaving is to be symbolic of the proletariat or world upheaval. And it is likewise to be symbolic of the subconscious penetration of the conscious mind."[5]

Even in the late 1920s, Toomer would write of how existing economic, political, and social systems formed the ground of racial division and exploitation. Yet racial modes of thinking and feeling had taken on a semiautonomous life of their own that prevented any intelligent grappling with the basic inequities of modern society and merely contributed to the trap in which all Americans were caught. To Toomer, the answer was to combat "mutually repellent" psychological tendencies among different groups. He turned increasingly to psychological and spiritual exploration, guided in part by a theory about the emergence of a new "American" race, of which he considered himself the first conscious member. Spiritual and psychological transformation, Toomer believed, would be the first step toward social reconstruction. Maybe a radically experimental literature could inspire this step.

Between 1919 and 1929 political conservatism and reaction had driven many left-wing artists to cultural radicalism, psychological and "spiritual" programs to transform society. Waldo Frank, already an important voice on the left, published *Our America* just as Toomer's first pieces appeared in the *Call*, complementing the direction in which Toomer was moving. Soon the two men would meet, and in short order were addressing each other as "brother." In Frank's vision, young writers and artists were to play a crucial role in bringing a new America into being. Believing that "Puritan" and "pioneer" traditions had prevented the emergence of a genuine American culture, Frank argued that the United States had no rooted peasant traditions out of which a national art might develop. The social elite looked to imported culture as a mark of status, and the immigrant working classes had discarded what spiritual heritage they had brought with them in the mad dash for "Americanization." Anglo-Americans had never put down roots in the continent, and the cultures of the Indian and Mexican had succumbed to white, industrial civilization. Thus the American people were reduced to automatons serving capitalist overlords and their machines. Industrialism and materialism rendered the nation a cultural and spiritual waste-land. Yet Frank believed the "American chaos" would finally give birth to a living culture. The "spiritual pioneers" of the rising generation would move beyond naturalism and critical realism to a fusion of the revolutionist and the artist-prophet in the "bringer of a new religion."[6]

Like most white intellectuals of the time, Frank failed to take any notice of African American culture, as Toomer would point out to him in 1922. W. E. B. Du Bois had proclaimed as early as 1903 that black Americans offered the only indigenous spirituality, the only folk song and simple reverence, the only genuine "culture" in a "dusty desert of dollars and smartness."[7]

Just as he tended later in life to downplay the influence of socialism on his thinking, Toomer covered up much of his apparent indebtedness to African American thought in his early intellectual development. He clearly had read Du Bois, for example. The controversy between Du Bois and Booker T. Washington (who had occasionally stayed at the Pinch-back home) would surely have been a topic of conversation within his family, and the way in which he imagined African American culture transforming Frank's cultural nationalist program seems to owe much to Du Bois's *The Souls of Black Folk*. Alain Locke, a philosophy professor at Howard University, knew Toomer by at least 1919 and acted as an early adviser. He may have been the first person with whom Toomer shared some of the pieces that went into *Cane*. Locke's ideas had been developing along lines parallel to Van Wyck Brooks's and Waldo Frank's since at least 1911. In his foreword to the famous anthology *The New Negro* (1925), a key text of the Harlem Renaissance, Locke would connect the Negro's "spiritual coming of age" with what Brooks (his Harvard class-mate) had termed "America's coming of age": "The New

Negro must be seen in the perspective of a New World, and especially of a New America. . . . America seeking a new spiritual expansion and artistic maturity, trying to found an American literature, a national art, and national music implies a Negro-American culture seeking the same satisfactions and objectives."[8]

The poet Georgia Douglas Johnson was also an important contact and source of moral support before Toomer had connected with white modernists. She expressed approval for how much he had "improved" through his contact with New York intellectuals. Toomer directed study sessions at Johnson's home on the history of slavery, the social and economic forces behind racial ideology, and the position of the "mixed race group" in the United States. At about this time Johnson wrote her own poems of the "new race," which would appear in the climactic section of her book *Bronze*. The sessions initiated by Toomer apparently formed the beginning of her regular "Saturday nighters"—meetings of black writers and intellectuals interested in contemporary issues and literature. These helped incubate what came to be called the Negro Renaissance. Thus Toomer drew on two different communities of thinking, roughly centered in black Washington and Greenwich Village, in the years immediately preceding *Cane*.

Through his grandfather's contacts, Toomer accepted a short-term position as substitute principal of Sparta Agricultural and Industrial Institute, beginning in September 1921. Located a mile or so outside Sparta (the Sempter of *Cane*) in east central Georgia, the school trained young black men and women chiefly for jobs in agriculture and light industry. Toomer spent only two months there before the principal returned, but the experience was pivotal. It exposed him for the first time to southern folk music in its native setting. Yet, the fact that black townspeople disdained the music as "shouting" only confirmed his belief that the folk culture would soon die out in the "modern desert." He wished to preserve it while there was still time. The experience in Sparta unleashed a steady creative surge.

Toomer found Washington superficially stagnant, but the life of Seventh Street, where black migrants settled and re-created themselves as an urban working class, now captured his attention in a new way. It seemed to Toomer to express a stage in the ultimate "absorption" of the folk spirit into the modern "chaos," at the same time transforming the dominant culture. Northern and "educated" African Americans, he noted, disdained the black folk culture and worshipped an "Anglo-Saxon ideal"; he wanted to awaken them to the beauty of "mellowed cadences" and "the charm of soft full lines. Of dusk faces. Of crisp curly hair." They must "create a living ideal of their own"—a black aesthetic, so to speak.[9]

Toomer considered this a step en route to a more encompassing American ideal, of which he believed himself the prophet. He wrote the editors of *The Liberator*, "From my own point of view I am naturally and inevitably an American. I have striven for a spiritual fusion analogous to the fact of racial intermingling. Without denying a single element in me, with no desire to subdue, one to the other, I have sought to let them function as complements." His "growing need for artistic expression" had pulled him "deeper and deeper into the Negro group. And as my powers of receptivity increased, I found myself loving it in a way that I could never love the other. It has stimulated and fertilized whatever creative talent I may contain within me."[10] In a letter from December of the same year (1922), Toomer wrote Sherwood Anderson that he believed his work would "aid in giving the Negro to himself" and proposed a new magazine, one that would "consciously hoist, and perhaps at first a trifle over emphasize a negroid ideal."[11] Yet he was disappointed when Anderson responded to him as a Negro. To Toomer, when the Negro ideal had achieved its full development, transforming all Americans, it would help usher in a new and greater ideal—an ideal for which he was a sort of John the Baptist.

Toomer took a second trip south with the Jewish Waldo Frank, who "passed" as black so that they could travel and eat together while feeling the pressure of segregation, as Frank worked on the novel *Holiday*; the two men began thinking of their books as interrelated efforts to bring the South to artistic fruition. Upon returning to Washington, Toomer took a job for two weeks as assistant manager at the Howard Theater, a popular black-managed theater in the heart of what later became known as Washington's "Little Harlem," where African American revues destined for fame in New York held trial runs. This experience inspired "Theater" and "Box Seat." Toomer remained in contact with Alain Locke, who helped him place "Song of the Son" in *The Crisis*, associated with the NAACP. Thereafter, other pieces from what is now *Cane* began appearing in "little magazines" associated with left-wing politics and the modernist avant-garde.

Toomer had read Sherwood Anderson's *Winesburg, Ohio* and *Triumph of the Egg and Other Stories* just before going to Sparta and asserted that these books had nourished his artistic response to the folk life there. His sketches owed much to Anderson's method of deemphasizing plot and developing instead a "lyric fiction," using repetition and refrain to structure the work. Each sketch thus came to have an essentially musical or poetic structure. Interspersed poems and songs also give a basal rhythm and mood to a story or sketch.

Like *Winesburg*, the first and last sections of *Cane* (which Toomer initially planned to form the whole of the book) presented a series of semi-independent stories or sketches, focusing on different characters, all set in the same locale. A sense of spiritual and emotional frustration, failure of basic communication between individuals, and repression of natural energies suffuses the book, revealing the chaos of contemporary American life and the need for a spiritual awakening, a bursting of unconscious forces through the crust of worn-out traditions. In *Cane*, these forces are distinctly black, and politically volatile.

Toomer aspired to go beyond Anderson and Waldo Frank, moreover, in response to the forces of industrialization and modern technology. The introduction of the machine, he believed, had destroyed humanity's balance with nature, creating spiritual conflicts to which artists had responded either by rejecting "the Machine" and suggesting back-to-nature programs or by accepting the machine as a necessary evil and creating aesthetic "counter-forms" against its destructive features. The former car salesman proposed instead that artists must create new forms that would spiritualize machinery and absorb its power. Toomer would install dynamos in his prose, electrical wiring in his poetry. Hence such pieces as "Her Lips Are Copper Wire" in the second section of *Cane*, which use the new machine forces as potentially positive metaphors of human connection: "with your tongue remove the tape / and press your lips to mine / till they are incandescent."

Toomer aspired to a "classic American prose," a fusion of heterogeneous rhythms, words, and forms of pronunciation currently differentiated into conflicting racial and class dialects. Like jazz, slang and colloquialisms kept pace with the introduction of new forces into society; literary artists should do no less. Hence Kabnis's tortured attempt to find words to "feed his soul"—the soul of the South, fed by the words of "white folks" "black niggers," "yaller niggers": "This whole damn bloated purple country feeds it cause its goin down t hell in a holy avalanche of words. I want t feed the soul—I know what that is; the preachers dont—but I've got t feed it." Kabnis's need to create "golden words" to transmute the terrors of southern history into aesthetic value and spiritual awakening is Jean Toomer's as he worked toward his own voice under the pressure of southern life. But "Kabnis" ends before its central character achieves what Toomer and Waldo Frank would call "fusion." Toomer intended "Kabnis" as the dramatization of a phase from which both he and the United States were about to emerge. Thus he ends the book on a note of uncertainty, transition—rather than resolution and achieved identity in either comic or tragic mode.

Some notion of Frank's fictional method helps explain aspects of Toomer's book, particularly its second section and its overall design. Toomer wrote Gorham Munson in October 1922 that, except for Anderson earlier, "(and to a lesser extent Frost and Sandburg) Waldo is the only modern writer who has immediately influenced me. He is so powerful and close, he has so many elements that I need, that I would be afraid of downright imitation if I were not so sure of myself."[12] Particularly in such narratives as "Theater," "Box Seat," and "Kabnis" (which is dedicated to Frank), Toomer structured the plot around "slopes," "curves," and "crescendos" of cognition, physical action, and emotion, to use the contemporary lingo of Frank, Munson, and Toomer. Swift, dramatic shifts, soliloquies in rapid transit between different thoughts, moods, and physical impressions were to suggest a dynamic structure and explosive forces, with chaotic fluxes terminating in decisive statements. The effect was to be kaleidoscopic. "Lyrical crystallizations" would bring several moving elements of a piece to a sudden, brilliant integration, as when, in "Box Seat," for example, a jagged series of interpenetrating actions, thoughts, and statements by different characters ends with the character Dan Moore suddenly crying out, "JESUS WAS ONCE A LEPER!"

Toomer believed the larger structure of a work should be itself a "lyric crystallization of which the interior poems and images are the facets." The overall structure of a work should have an underlying spherical form, with a curve cementing the various parts together and "giving the Whole a dynamic propulsion forward," to borrow from Toomer's own phrasing with regard to Frank's novels *Rahab* and *City Block*.[13] In a letter to Frank, Toomer noted that "from three angles, *Cane*'s design is a circle. Aesthetically, from simple forms to complex ones, and back to simple forms. Regionally, from the South up into the North, and back into the South again. Or, from the North down into the South, and then a return North. From the point of view of the spiritual entity behind the work [that is, Toomer's own spiritual development], the curve really starts with Bona and Paul (awakening), plunges into Kabnis, emerges in Karintha etc. swings upward into Theatre [sic] and Box Seat, and ends (pauses) in Harvest Song."[14] To reinforce the design, Toomer included a series of arcs before the three divisions of the book.

His more complex tales and dramatic sketches differentiate characters in relation to the multiple dimensions of human consciousness that affect their actions. Because of the disintegrating forces of modern society, these different dimensions—intellection, physical passion, emotion, and dream—rarely achieve integration either within or between individuals. In "Theater," for example, Dorris and John fail to coincide emotionally and complement each other, largely because of class differences that block communication and because they do not have a proper balance of physical, intellectual, verbal, and emotional capacities. John is overly intellectual; Dorris, openly passionate and physical, suspects him of being "dictie."

The frustration of many characters in *Cane* owes much to the chaotic and unsatisfying state of male-female relationships. Toomer's personal ideal for the relationship between a man and a woman stressed inherent differences between them, with the woman often in the role of muse and pupil, inspirer of the male prophet-creator. Men, Toomer believed, are dynamic and aggressive by nature; women, primarily lyrical and receptive. Both are incomplete in themselves. Yet Toomer is capable of endowing some of his female characters, such as Carma, with remarkable strength, and in much of *Cane* female sexuality either overpowers or nearly overpowers the male characters. The man must control his responses, be attentive to woman's needs, and lead the relationship toward a "fusion" of complementary elements.

Nonetheless, *Cane* also reveals the damage done to women by the restriction of their lives, particularly through men's use of them as mere vessels of meaning, routes to higher consciousness, or means of sexual satisfaction—roles that women often played in Toomer's own life. *Cane* critiques its narrators' own ambivalence about female sexuality, an insecurity about masculine identity at the heart of the desire for fusion of male and female energies. A desire for domination and control competes and is thoroughly intertwined with a desire of the male to lose himself in the sublime embrace of the female. It is difficult not to notice a correspondence in the book between this complex of masculine desire and the ambiguity of racial and class identities with their frustrated or repressed longing for self-transcendence. Such transcendence Toomer associated with spiritual "fruition," an ecstatic transformation of human being.

Cane, while a critical success, sold well below a thousand copies, and Toomer never composed the books he had planned and described to Liveright, his publisher, as Cane was in press. He had come to believe that the literary vocation in its current state was part of the problem of modernity rather than a solution. The artist must learn to unify himself before attempting to provide a new vision for society. An old "slope" of consciousness needed to be dissolved through spiritual self-development and then the seeds planted for a new one. Toomer turned to G. I. Gurdjieff's program the Harmonious Development of Man, which had much in common with beliefs Toomer already held about the need for a balance of intellectual, emotional, and instinctual aspects of the self. (He was not alone: many other writers and artists took the same direction at this time.) His disaffection with the literary vocation seems intimately intertwined with a sense of his failure to free words from limiting forms of consciousness and social institutions—including the institution of race.

The drama surrounding the publication of Cane epitomizes the fact that no person considered "Negro," according to the one-drop rule of the United States, could get a hearing except under the sign of blackness, even if they did not consider themselves black. Horace Liveright probably was interested in the book partly because it was by someone he considered black. He considered the race of the author crucial to marketing Cane. Toomer objected, and Liveright (who was Jewish) then expressed wonder that he would wish to "dodge" the fact of his racial identity, infuriating the author. Nonetheless, washing his hands of the advertising program, Toomer explicitly allowed Liveright to "feature Negro" if he wished, while insisting that any representation of the book to reviewers and the like and anything purporting to reflect Toomer's own views must not refer to him as a Negro but reflect his own "fundamental position." "My racial composition and my position in the world are realities which I alone may determine. . . . I expect and demand acceptance of myself on their basis. I do not expect to be told what I should consider myself to be."[15]

He had made that position known to the head of the Associated Negro Press well before *Cane*'s publication. Responding to Claude Barnett's inquiry about his racial identity, Toomer replied, "The true and complete answer is one of some complexity, and for this reason perhaps it will not be seen and accepted until after I am dead. . . . The answer involves a realistic and accurate knowledge of racial mixture, of nationality as formed by the interaction of tradition, culture, and environment, of the artistic nature in its relation to the racial or social group, etc. All of which of course is too heavy and thick to go into now. Let me state then, simply, that I am the grandson of the late P. B. S. Pinchback. From this fact it is clear that . . . I have 'peeped behind the veil.' And my deepest impulse to literature (on the side of material) is the direct result of what I saw."[16] Contrary to some later narratives, Toomer was not attempting to "pass" as white. He would adhere to his own self-understanding while allowing others to make of him what they would. He considered himself the first conscious member of a "new race" coming into existence in the United States, and *Cane* itself attests pervasively to this idea, in that it presents a cycle of history coming to a close, awaiting the birth of a new one. *Cane*, he famously insisted, was a "swan song."

Being identified as a Negro author would not only violate Toomer's philosophy and personal self-conception but would also lead people to interpret his work entirely in relation to issues of racial identity, as "Negro literature." Toomer wrote that whatever promotional statements he made about *Cane* would "inevitably come from a synthetic human and art point of view, not a racial one."[17] He fully realized that his self-definition would lead many people to the same conclusion as Liveright—that he was dodging his racial identity. Yet he could hardly pass as white in the conventional sense, even if he wanted to. In fact, reporters in Wisconsin picked up on his first marriage to a white woman and made much ballyhoo about it, while he insisted that it was the marriage of two "Americans." Many of Toomer's black readers and white friends already thought of him as a Negro, knew his family as a Negro family, and would not have understood his self-description any more than Horace Liveright did. He neither cut off such friends nor avoided other African Americans. Quite the contrary, in addition to starting a Gurdjieff group composed mostly of African American artists and friends, he continued to have black friends visit him in Greenwich Village. Toomer's notes for the meetings he led in New York show that he gave advice to aspiring black creative writers and encouraged artistic experimentation. According to Aaron Douglas, the marquee artist of the Harlem Renaissance, Toomer taught "that we all have the potentialities of intellectual, artistic giants if we could only get to the bottom of our real selves. He claims that back deep in our natures there is a mine of unused power, a source, a hitherto little known faculty which is neither body, emotion nor intellect, but is equal to the combined power of all. The key to this source is self-observation. The ultimate goal is free will."[18]

In 1925, Toomer gave a lecture at the 135th Street branch of the New York Public Library (the intellectual hub of black Harlem), "Towards Reality," in which he greeted the budding Negro Renaissance as "evidence of a two-fold fact, the fact that the Negro is in the process of discovering himself, and of being discovered" by the culturally aware members of the white world. "I would be receptive of his reality as it emerges," he concluded, "(being active only by way of aid to this emergence), assured that in proportion as he discovers what is real within him, he will create, and by that act create at once himself and contribute his value to America."[19] This was hardly the act of a black man attempting to pass as white. The black Harlem newspapers reported on the event to a readership that thought of Toomer as a Negro. The white editor John Farrar, who also thought of Toomer as a Negro, reported on the event for the *Bookman*, finding the lecture a bit too "abstruse."[20]

Alas, it was one thing for Toomer to work out a position in his own mind and to share it with his friends. It was quite another to project his concept into "this American world in which, as I had come to realize more and more, there was this fixed view that in this country a person must be either black or white."[21] When faced with official government forms, which did not allow for his self-identity, he would identify himself or be identified as "Negro" or "White," but this did not signal the adequacy of such labels.[22] As Allyson Hobbs has argued in an award-winning history of passing in the United States, Toomer was not "confused, racially misidentified, or frustrated with the limits of language, but rather struggling to convey a holistic understanding" in a society that would not, and still cannot, accept that understanding.[23]

None of Toomer's seeming compromises about letting people come to their own conclusions about his racial identity contradict his commitment, however utopian, to the idea of a new race. *Cane* is full of inarticulate members of this new group of "Americans" (both black and white) who have yet to become "conscious" of themselves, in Toomer's phrasing. It presents others in whom violation of the color line provokes ostracism or death as Americans resist the "merging," haunted by wraiths of the past and established socioeconomic structures. This feature of his book remained illegible to critics for more than half a century.

Americans were not going in Toomer's direction. Indeed, the great irony of his career is that modern American racial discourse—with an absolute polarity between white and black at its center—took its most definite shape precisely during the course of his life. The United States would be more segregated at the time of Toomer's death than it had been at the time of his birth, despite the dismantling of some of the legal bulwarks of white supremacy. The "mulatto" designation disappeared from the U.S. Census in 1920. Only in 2000 could people choose to mark more than one racial box on the census forms. Toomer probably would have found even this misguided.

It is a sign of the fundamentally segregated nature of American society that *Cane* could only be understood as a black text and in relation to African American identity. Toomer's connection with the Harlem Renaissance largely accounts for the availability of his work today. Georgia O'Keeffe (with whom Toomer had had an affair in the 1920s) and Toomer's former white roommate at the University of Wisconsin wanted to bring it out in the 1950s, when Toomer also renewed his copyright, but only after he died was the book reissued, in the context of the "black aesthetic." Interest in African American literature, and the Harlem Renaissance in particular, brought *Cane* back to public attention—and into print—some forty years after its second small printing.

It must be allowed that Toomer would be upset; it must also be allowed that this connection is not inappropriate. Not only was *Cane* a tremendous influence upon the Harlem

Renaissance and later African American writing, it was produced by the same confluence of institutions and even individuals that helped produce the Harlem Renaissance. But while it is entirely fitting to read *Cane* in the context of African American literary tradition, it is just as important to recognize that it can be read in relation to other traditions and movements. Indeed, it is precisely the liminality—and mobility—of Toomer's identity in a society obsessed with clarity on this score that motivated the restless searching through which *Cane* came about, through which Toomer left it behind, and without which there could be no book like it.

GEORGE HUTCHINSON

Suggestions for Further Reading

Casey Nelson Blake, *Beloved Community: The Cultural Criticism of Randolph Bourne, Van Wyck Brooks, Waldo Frank, and Lewis Mumford*. Chapel Hill: University of North Carolina Press, 1990.

Rudolph P. Byrd. *Jean Toomer's Years with Gurdjieff: Portrait of an Artist, 1923–1936*. Athens: University of Georgia Press, 1990.

Geneviève Fabre and Michel Feith, eds. *Jean Toomer and the Harlem Renaissance*. New Brunswick, NJ: Rutgers University Press, 2001.

Barbara Foley. *Jean Toomer: Race, Repression, and Revolution*. Urbana: University of Illinois Press, 2014.

———. "Jean Toomer's Sparta." *American Literature* 6 (1995): 4–5.

Allyson Hobbs. *A Chosen Exile: A History of Racial Passing in American History*. Cambridge, MA: Harvard University Press, 2014.

George Hutchinson. *The Harlem Renaissance in Black and White*. Cambridge, MA: Harvard University Press, 1995.

———. "Jean Toomer and American Racial Discourse." *Texas Studies in Literature and Language* 35, no. 2 (1993): 226–50.

Robert B. Jones, ed. *Jean Toomer: Selected Essays and Literary Criticism*. Knoxville: University of Tennessee Press, 1996.

———. *Jean Toomer and the Prison-House of Thought: A Phenomenology of the Spirit*. Amherst: University of Massachusetts Press, 1993.

Cynthia Earl Kerman and Richard Eldridge. *The Lives of Jean Toomer: A Hunger for Wholeness*. Baton Rouge: Louisiana State University Press, 1987.

Alain Locke, ed. *The New Negro: An Interpretation*. New York: Boni & Liveright, 1925.

Frederik L. Rusch, ed. *A Jean Toomer Reader: Selected Unpublished Writings*. New York: Oxford University Press, 1993.

Charles Scruggs and Lee VanDemarr. *Jean Toomer and the Terrors of American History*. Philadelphia: Pennsylvania University Press, 1998.

Jean Toomer. *The Collected Poems of Jean Toomer*. Ed. Robert B. Jones and Margery Toomer Latimer. Chapel Hill: University of North Carolina Press, 1988.

Darwin T. Turner, ed. *The Wayward and the Seeking: A Collection of Writings by Jean Toomer*. Washington, DC: Howard University Press, 1980.

Mark Whalan, ed. *The Letters of Jean Toomer, 1919–1924*. Knoxville: University of Tennessee Press, 2006.

———. *Race, Manhood, and Modernism in America: The Short Story Cycles of Sherwood Anderson and Jean Toomer*. Knoxville: University of Tennessee Press, 2007.

A Note on the Text

The text used for this edition of *Cane* is the first edition, first printing, by Boni & Liveright, 1923. The second printing (1927) was identical to the first, as was the third, published in 1967 after Toomer's death—with the exception that in the third printing the arc appearing on the page before "Karintha" was unaccountably dropped. Toomer clearly had nothing to do with this omission. I have made few editorial corrections—for example, of "cane-brake" to "canebrake" on its first appearance, thus bringing it into conformity with subsequent spellings in the text; and of "overhead" (clearly a typographical slip) to "overheard" in the story "Avey." Other probably typographical errors I have let stand, but with notes suggesting the likely alternatives.

This Penguin Classics edition restores Toomer's epigraph, which appeared in the editions he oversaw. It also restores his note of thanks to the magazines in which his pieces first appeared. In Appendix I, I have provided accurate bibliographical information for the first magazine publication history of pieces that Toomer included in *Cane*. Appendix II presents Waldo Frank's foreword to the first edition.

Cane

Oracular.
Redolent of fermenting syrup,
Purple of the dusk,
Deep-rooted cane.[1]

To my grandmother . . .

Certain of these pieces have appeared in *Broom*, *Crisis*, *Double Dealer*, *Liberator*, *Little Review*, *Modern Review*, *Nomad*, *Prairie*, and *S4N*.

To these magazines: thanks.

KARINTHA

Her skin is like dusk on the eastern horizon,
O cant you see it, O cant you see it,
Her skin is like dusk on the eastern horizon
. . . When the sun goes down.

Men had always wanted her, this Karintha, even as a child,
Karintha carrying beauty, perfect as dusk when the sun goes
down. Old men rode her hobby-horse upon their knees.
Young men danced with her at frolics when they should have
been dancing with their grownup girls. God grant us youth,
secretly prayed the old men. The young fellows counted the
time to pass before she would be old enough to mate with
them. This interest of the male, who wishes to ripen a growing thing too soon, could mean no good to her.

Karintha, at twelve, was a wild flash that told the other
folks just what it was to live. At sunset, when there was no
wind, and the pine-smoke from over by the sawmill hugged
the earth, and you couldnt see more than a few feet in front,
her sudden darting past you was a bit of vivid color, like a
black bird that flashes in light. With the other children one
could hear, some distance off, their feet flopping in the

two-inch dust. Karintha's running was a whir. It had the
sound of the red dust that sometimes makes a spiral in the
road. At dusk, during the hush just after the sawmill had
closed down, and before any of the women had started their
supper-getting-ready songs, her voice, high-pitched, shrill,
would put one's ears to itching. But no one ever thought to
make her stop because of it. She stoned the cows, and beat
her dog, and fought the other children . . . Even the preacher,
who caught her at mischief, told himself that she was as innocently lovely as a November cotton flower. Already, rumors were out about her. Homes in Georgia are most often
built on the two-room plan. In one, you cook and eat, in the
other you sleep, and there love goes on. Karintha had seen or
heard, perhaps she had felt her parents loving. One could but
imitate one's parents, for to follow them was the way of God.
She played "home" with a small boy who was not afraid to
do her bidding. That started the whole thing. Old men could
no longer ride her hobby-horse upon their knees. But young
men counted faster.

> Her skin is like dusk,
> O cant you see it,
> Her skin is like dusk,
> When the sun goes down.

Karintha is a woman. She who carries beauty, perfect as
dusk when the sun goes down. She has been married many
times. Old men remind her that a few years back they rode
her hobby-horse upon their knees. Karintha smiles, and in-
dulges them when she is in the mood for it. She has contempt
for them. Karintha is a woman. Young men run stills[1] to
make her money. Young men go to the big cities and run on
the road. Young men go away to college. They all want to

bring her money. These are the young men who thought that all they had to do was to count time. But Karintha is a woman, and she has had a child. A child fell out of her womb onto a bed of pine-needles in the forest. Pine-needles are smooth and sweet. They are elastic to the feet of rabbits . . . A sawmill was nearby. Its pyramidal sawdust pile smouldered. It is a year before one completely burns. Meanwhile, the smoke curls up and hangs in odd wraiths about the trees, curls up, and spreads itself out over the valley . . . Weeks after Karintha returned home the smoke was so heavy you tasted it in water. Some one made a song:

> Smoke is on the hills. Rise up.
> Smoke is on the hills, O rise
> And take my soul to Jesus.

Karintha is a woman. Men do not know that the soul of her was a growing thing ripened too soon. They will bring their money; they will die not having found it out . . . Karintha at twenty, carrying beauty, perfect as dusk when the sun goes down. Karintha . . .

> Her skin is like dusk on the eastern horizon,
> O cant you see it, O cant you see it,
> Her skin is like dusk on the eastern horizon
> . . . When the sun goes down.

> Goes down . . .

REAPERS

Black reapers with the sound of steel on stones
Are sharpening scythes. I see them place the hones
In their hip-pockets as a thing that's done,
And start their silent swinging, one by one.
Black horses drive a mower through the weeds,
And there, a field rat, startled, squealing bleeds,
His belly close to ground. I see the blade,
Blood-stained, continue cutting weeds and shade.

NOVEMBER COTTON FLOWER

Boll-weevil's coming,[1] and the winter's cold,
Made cotton-stalks look rusty, seasons old,
And cotton, scarce as any southern snow,
Was vanishing; the branch, so pinched and slow,
Failed in its function as the autumn rake;
Drouth fighting soil had caused the soil to take
All water from the streams; dead birds were found
In wells a hundred feet below the ground—
Such was the season when the flower bloomed.
Old folks were startled, and it soon assumed
Significance. Superstition saw
Something it had never seen before:
Brown eyes that loved without a trace of fear,
Beauty so sudden for that time of year.

BECKY

Becky was the white woman who had two Negro sons.
She's dead; they've gone away. The pines whisper to Jesus.
The Bible flaps its leaves with an aimless rustle on her
mound.

Becky had one Negro son. Who gave it to her? Damn buck
nigger, said the white folks' mouths. She wouldnt tell. Common, God-forsaken, insane white shameless wench, said the
white folks' mouths. Her eyes were sunken, her neck stringy,
her breasts fallen, till then. Taking their words, they filled
her, like a bubble rising—then she broke. Mouth setting in a
twist that held her eyes, harsh, vacant, staring . . . Who gave
it to her? Low-down nigger with no self-respect, said the
black folks' mouths. She wouldnt tell. Poor Catholic poor-
white crazy woman, said the black folks' mouths. White
folks and black folks built her cabin, fed her and her growing
baby, prayed secretly to God who'd put His cross upon her
and cast her out.

When the first was born, the white folks said they'd have
no more to do with her. And black folks, they too joined
hands to cast her out . . . The pines whispered to Jesus. . The

railroad boss said not to say he said it, but she could live, if she wanted to, on the narrow strip of land between the railroad and the road. John Stone, who owned the lumber and the bricks, would have shot the man who told he gave the stuff to Lonnie Deacon, who stole out there at night and built the cabin. A single room held down to earth . . . O fly away to Jesus . . . by a leaning chimney . . .

Six trains each day rumbled past and shook the ground under her cabin. Fords, and horse- and mule-drawn buggies went back and forth along the road. No one ever saw her. Trainmen, and passengers who'd heard about her, threw out papers and food. Threw out little crumpled slips of paper scribbled with prayers, as they passed her eye-shaped piece of sandy ground. Ground islandized between the road and railroad track. Pushed up where a blue-sheen God with listless eyes could look at it. Folks from the town took turns, unknown, of course, to each other, in bringing corn and meat and sweet potatoes. Even sometimes snuff . . . O thank y Jesus . . . Old David Georgia, grinding cane and boiling syrup, never went her way without some sugar sap. No one ever saw her. The boy grew up and ran around. When he was five years old as folks reckoned it, Hugh Jourdon saw him carrying a baby. "Becky has another son," was what the whole town knew. But nothing was said, for the part of man that says things to the likes of that had told itself that if there was a Becky, that Becky now was dead.

The two boys grew. Sullen and cunning . . . O pines, whisper to Jesus; tell Him to come and press sweet Jesus-lips against their lips and eyes . . . It seemed as though with those two big fellows there, there could be no room for Becky. The part that prayed wondered if perhaps she'd really died, and they had buried her. No one dared ask. They'd beat and cut a man who meant nothing at all in mentioning that they lived along the road. White or colored? No one knew, and least of all themselves. They drifted around from job to job. We, who had cast out their mother because of them, could we take them in? They answered black and white folks by shooting up two men and leaving town. "Godam the white folks; godam the niggers," they shouted as they left town. Becky? Smoke curled up from her chimney; she must be there. Trains passing shook the ground. The ground shook the leaning chimney. Nobody noticed it. A creepy feeling came over all who saw that thin wraith of smoke and felt the trembling of the ground. Folks began to take her food again. They quit it soon because they had a fear. Becky if dead might be a hant,[1] and if alive—it took some nerve even to mention it . . . O pines, whisper to Jesus . . .

It was Sunday. Our congregation had been visiting at Pulverton, and were coming home. There was no wind. The autumn sun, the bell from Ebenezer Church, listless and heavy. Even the pines were stale, sticky, like the smell of food that makes you sick. Before we turned the bend of the road that would show us the Becky cabin, the horses stopped stock-still, pushed back their ears, and nervously whinnied. We urged, then whipped them on. Quarter of a mile away thin smoke curled up from the leaning chimney . . . O pines, whisper to Jesus . . . Goose-flesh came on my skin though there still was neither chill nor wind. Eyes left their sockets for the cabin. Ears burned and throbbed. Uncanny eclipse! fear closed my mind. We were just about to pass . . . Pines shout to Jesus! . . the ground trembled as a ghost train rumbled by. The chimney fell into the cabin. Its thud was like a hollow report, ages having passed since it went off. Barlo and I were pulled out of our seats.

Dragged to the door that had swung open. Through the dust we saw the bricks in a mound upon the floor. Becky, if she was there, lay under them. I thought I heard a groan. Barlo, mumbling something, threw his Bible on the pile. (No one has ever touched it.) Somehow we got away. My buggy was still on the road. The last thing that I remember was whipping old Dan like fury; I remember nothing after that—that is, until I reached town and folks crowded round to get the true word of it.

Becky was the white woman who had two Negro sons. She's dead; they've gone away. The pines whisper to Jesus. The Bible flaps its leaves with an aimless rustle on her mound.

FACE

Hair—
silver-gray,
like streams of stars,
Brows—
recurved canoes
quivered by the ripples blown by pain,
Her eyes—
mist of tears
condensing on the flesh below
And her channeled muscles
are cluster grapes of sorrow
purple in the evening sun
nearly ripe for worms.

COTTON SONG

Come, brother, come. Lets lift it;
Come now, hewit! roll away!
Shackles fall upon the Judgment Day
But lets not wait for it.

God's body's got a soul,
Bodies like to roll the soul,
Cant blame God if we dont roll,
Come, brother, roll, roll!

Cotton bales are the fleecy way
Weary sinner's bare feet trod,
Softly, softly to the throne of God,
"We aint agwine t wait until th Judgment Day!

Nassur; nassur,
Hump.
Eoho, eoho, roll away!
We aint agwine t wait until th Judgment Day!"

God's body's got a soul,
Bodies like to roll the soul,
Cant blame God if we dont roll,
Come, brother, roll, roll!

CARMA[1]

Wind is in the cane. Come along.
Cane leaves swaying, rusty with talk,
Scratching choruses above the guinea's squawk,[2]
Wind is in the cane. Come along.

Carma, in overalls, and strong as any man, stands behind the old brown mule, driving the wagon home. It bumps, and groans, and shakes as it crosses the railroad track. She, riding it easy. I leave the men around the stove to follow her with my eyes down the red dust road. Nigger woman driving a Georgia chariot down an old dust road. Dixie Pike is what they call it. Maybe she feels my gaze, perhaps she expects it. Anyway, she turns. The sun, which has been slanting over her shoulder, shoots primitive rockets into her mangrove-gloomed, yellow flower face. Hi! Yip! God has left the Moses-people for the nigger. "Gedap." Using reins to slap the mule, she disappears in a cloudy rumble at some indefinite point along the road.

(The sun is hammered to a band of gold. Pine-needles, like mazda,[3] are brilliantly aglow. No rain has come to take the rustle from the falling sweet-gum leaves. Over in the forest, across the swamp, a sawmill blows its closing whistle. Smoke curls up. Marvelous web spun by the spider sawdust pile. Curls up and spreads itself pine-high above the branch, a single silver band along the eastern valley. A black boy . . . you are the most sleepiest man I ever seed, Sleeping Beauty . . . cradled on a gray mule, guided by the hollow sound of cowbells, heads for them through a rusty cotton field. From down the railroad track, the chugchug of a gas engine announces that the repair gang is coming home. A girl in the yard of a whitewashed shack not much larger than the stack of worn ties piled before it, sings. Her voice is loud. Echoes, like rain, sweep the valley. Dusk takes the polish from the rails. Lights twinkle in scattered houses. From far away, a sad strong song. Pungent and composite, the smell of farmyards is the fragrance of the woman. She does not sing; her body is a song. She is in the forest, dancing. Torches flare . . juju men, greegree,[4] witch-doctors . . torches go out . . . The Dixie Pike has grown from a goat path in Africa.

NIGHT.

Foxie, the bitch, slicks back her ears and barks at the rising moon.)

> Wind is in the corn. Come along.
> Corn leaves swaying, rusty with talk,
> Scratching choruses above the guinea's squawk,
> Wind is in the corn. Come along.

Carma's tale is the crudest melodrama. Her husband's in the gang.[5] And its her fault he got there. Working with a contractor, he was away most of the time. She had others. No one blames her for that. He returned one day and hung around the town where he picked up week-old boasts and rumors . . . Bane accused her. She denied. He couldnt see that she was becoming hysterical. He would have liked to take his fists and beat her. Who was strong as a man. Stronger. Words, like corkscrews, wormed to her strength. It fizzled out. Grabbing a gun, she rushed from the house and plunged across the road into a canebrake. .[6] There, in quarter heaven shone the crescent moon . . . Bane was afraid to follow till he heard the gun go off. Then he wasted half an hour gathering the neighbor men. They met in the road where lamp-light showed tracks dissolving in the loose earth about the cane. The search began. Moths flickered the lamps. They put them out. Really, because she still might be live enough to shoot. Time and space have no meaning in a canefield. No more than the interminable stalks . . . Some one stumbled over her. A cry went up. From the road, one would have thought that they were cornering a rabbit or a skunk . . . It is difficult carrying dead weight through cane. They placed her on the sofa. A curious, nosey somebody looked for the wound. This fussing with her clothes aroused her. Her eyes were weak and pitiable for so strong a woman. Slowly, then like a flash, Bane came to know that the shot she fired, with averted head, was aimed to whistle like a dying hornet through the cane. Twice deceived, and one deception proved the other. His head went off. Slashed one of the men who'd helped, the man who'd stumbled over her. Now he's in the gang. Who was her husband. Should she not take others, this Carma, strong as a man, whose tale as I have told it is the crudest melodrama?

> Wind is in the cane. Come along.
> Cane leaves swaying, rusty with talk,
> Scratching choruses above the guinea's squawk,
> Wind is in the cane. Come along.

SONG OF THE SON

Pour O pour that parting soul in song,
O pour it in the sawdust glow of night,
Into the velvet pine-smoke air to-night,
And let the valley carry it along.
And let the valley carry it along.

O land and soil, red soil and sweet-gum tree,
So scant of grass, so profligate of pines,
Now just before an epoch's sun declines
Thy son, in time, I have returned to thee,
Thy son, I have in time returned to thee.

In time, for though the sun is setting on
A song-lit race of slaves, it has not set;
Though late, O soil, it is not too late yet
To catch thy plaintive soul, leaving, soon gone,
Leaving, to catch thy plaintive soul soon gone.

O Negro slaves, dark purple ripened plums,
Squeezed, and bursting in the pine-wood air,
Passing, before they stripped the old tree bare
One plum was saved for me, one seed becomes

An everlasting song, a singing tree,
Caroling softly souls of slavery,
What they were, and what they are to me,
Caroling softly souls of slavery.

GEORGIA DUSK

The sky, lazily disdaining to pursue
   The setting sun, too indolent to hold
   A lengthened tournament for flashing gold,
Passively darkens for night's barbecue,

A feast of moon and men and barking hounds,
   An orgy for some genius of the South
   With blood-hot eyes and cane-lipped scented mouth,
Surprised in making folk-songs from soul sounds.

The sawmill blows its whistle, buzz-saws stop,
   And silence breaks the bud of knoll and hill,
   Soft settling pollen where plowed lands fulfill
Their early promise of a bumper crop.

Smoke from the pyramidal sawdust pile
   Curls up, blue ghosts of trees, tarrying low
   Where only chips and stumps are left to show
The solid proof of former domicile.

Meanwhile, the men, with vestiges of pomp,
   Race memories of king and caravan,
   High-priests, an ostrich, and a juju-man,
Go singing through the footpaths of the swamp.

Their voices rise . . the pine trees are guitars,
   Strumming, pine-needles fall like sheets of rain . .
   Their voices rise . . the chorus of the cane
Is caroling a vesper[1] to the stars. .

O singers, resinous and soft your songs
   Above the sacred whisper of the pines,
   Give virgin lips to cornfield concubines,
Bring dreams of Christ to dusky cane-lipped throngs.

FERN

Face flowed into her eyes. Flowed in soft cream foam and plaintive ripples, in such a way that wherever your glance may momentarily have rested, it immediately thereafter wavered in the direction of her eyes. The soft suggestion of down slightly darkened, like the shadow of a bird's wing might, the creamy brown color of her upper lip. Why, after noticing it, you sought her eyes, I cannot tell you. Her nose was aquiline, Semitic. If you have heard a Jewish cantor[1] sing, if he has touched you and made your own sorrow seem trivial when compared with his, you will know my feeling when I follow the curves of her profile, like mobile rivers, to their common delta. They were strange eyes. In this, that they sought nothing—that is, nothing that was obvious and tangible and that one could see, and they gave the impression that nothing was to be denied. When a woman seeks, you will have observed, her eyes deny. Fern's eyes desired nothing that you could give her; there was no reason why they should withhold. Men saw her eyes and fooled themselves. Fern's eyes said to them that she was easy. When she was young, a few men took her, but got no joy from it. And then, once done, they felt bound to her (quite unlike their hit and run with other girls), felt as though it would take them a lifetime to fulfill an obligation which they could find no name for. They became attached to her, and hungered after finding the barest trace of what she might desire. As she grew up, new men who came to town felt as almost everyone did who ever saw her: that they would not be denied. Men were everlastingly bringing her their bodies. Something inside of her got tired of them, I guess, for I am certain that for the life of her she could not tell why or how she began to turn them off. A man in fever is no trifling thing to send away. They began to leave her, baffled and ashamed, yet vowing to themselves that some day they would do some fine thing for her: send her candy every week and not let her know whom it came from, watch out for her wedding-day and give her a magnificent something with no name on it, buy a house and deed it to her, rescue her from some unworthy fellow who had tricked her into marrying him. As you know, men are apt to idolize or fear that which they cannot understand, especially if it be a woman. She did not deny them, yet the fact was that they were denied. A sort of superstition crept into their consciousness of her being somehow above them. Being above them meant that she was not to be approached by anyone. She became a virgin. Now a virgin in a small southern town is by no means the usual thing, if you will believe me. That the sexes were made to mate is the practice of the South. Particularly, black folks were made to mate. And it is black folks whom I have been talking about thus far. What white men thought of Fern I can arrive at only by analogy. They let her alone.

Anyone, of course, could see her, could see her eyes. If you walked up the Dixie Pike most any time of day, you'd be most like to see her resting listless-like on the railing of her porch, back propped against a post, head tilted a little forward because there was a nail in the porch post just where

her head came which for some reason or other she never took
the trouble to pull out. Her eyes, if it were sunset, rested idly
where the sun, molten and glorious, was pouring down between the fringe of pines. Or maybe they gazed at the gray
cabin on the knoll from which an evening folk-song was
coming. Perhaps they followed a cow that had been turned
loose to roam and feed on cotton-stalks and corn leaves.
Like as not they'd settle on some vague spot above the horizon, though hardly a trace of wistfulness would come to
them. If it were dusk, then they'd wait for the search-light of
the evening train which you could see miles up the track before it flared across the Dixie Pike, close to her home. Wherever they looked, you'd follow them and then waver back.
Like her face, the whole countryside seemed to flow into her
eyes. Flowed into them with the soft listless cadence of Georgia's South. A young Negro, once, was looking at her, spell-
bound, from the road. A white man passing in a buggy had
to flick him with his whip if he was to get by without running him over. I first saw her on her porch. I was passing
with a fellow whose crusty numbness (I was from the North
and suspected of being prejudiced and stuck-up) was melting
as he found me warm. I asked him who she was. "That's
Fern," was all that I could get from him. Some folks already
thought that I was given to nosing around; I let it go at that,
so far as questions were concerned. But at first sight of her I
felt as if I heard a Jewish cantor sing. As if his singing rose
above the unheard chorus of a folk-song. And I felt bound to
her. I too had my dreams: something I would do for her. I
have knocked about from town to town too much not to
know the futility of mere change of place. Besides, picture if
you can, this cream-colored solitary girl sitting at a tenement
window looking down on the indifferent throngs of Harlem.
Better that she listen to folk-songs at dusk in Georgia, you

would say, and so would I. Or, suppose she came up North and married. Even a doctor or a lawyer, say, one who would be sure to get along—that is, make money. You and I know, who have had experience in such things, that love is not a thing like prejudice which can be bettered by changes of town. Could men in Washington, Chicago, or New York, more than the men of Georgia, bring her something left vacant by the bestowal of their bodies? You and I who know men in these cities will have to say, they could not. See her out and out a prostitute along State Street in Chicago.[2] See her move into a southern town where white men are more aggressive. See her become a white man's concubine . . . Something I must do for her. There was myself. What could I do for her? Talk, of course. Push back the fringe of pines upon new horizons. To what purpose? and what for? Her? Myself? Men in her case seem to lose their selfishness. I lost mine before I touched her. I ask you, friend (it makes no difference if you sit in the Pullman or the Jim Crow[3] as the train crosses her road), what thoughts would come to you— that is, after you'd finished with the thoughts that leap into men's minds at the sight of a pretty woman who will not deny them; what thoughts would come to you, had you seen her in a quick flash, keen and intuitively, as she sat there on her porch when your train thundered by? Would you have got off at the next station and come back for her to take her where? Would you have completely forgotten her as soon as you reached Macon, Atlanta, Augusta, Pasadena, Madison, Chicago, Boston, or New Orleans? Would you tell your wife or sweetheart about a girl you saw? Your thoughts can help me, and I would like to know. Something I would do for her . . .

One evening I walked up the Pike on purpose, and stopped to say hello. Some of her family were about, but they moved away to make room for me. Damn if I knew how to begin. Would you? Mr. and Miss So-and-So, people, the weather, the crops, the new preacher, the frolic, the church benefit, rabbit and possum hunting, the new soft drink they had at old Pap's store, the schedule of the trains, what kind of town Macon was, Negro's migration north, boll-weevils, syrup, the Bible—to all these things she gave a yassur or nassur, without further comment. I began to wonder if perhaps my own emotional sensibility had played one of its tricks on me. "Lets take a walk," I at last ventured. The suggestion, coming after so long an isolation, was novel enough, I guess, to surprise. But it wasnt that. Something told me that men before me had said just that as a prelude to the offering of their bodies. I tried to tell her with my eyes. I think she understood. The thing from her that made my throat catch, vanished. Its passing left her visible in a way I'd thought, but never seen. We walked down the Pike with people on all the porches gaping at us. "Doesnt it make you mad?" She meant the row of petty gossiping people. She meant the world. Through a canebrake that was ripe for cutting, the branch was reached. Under a sweet-gum tree, and where reddish leaves had dammed the creek a little, we sat down. Dusk, suggesting the almost imperceptible procession of giant trees, settled with a purple haze about the cane. I felt strange, as I always do in Georgia, particularly at dusk. I felt that things unseen to men were tangibly immediate. It would not have surprised me had I had vision. People have them in Georgia more often than you would suppose. A black woman once saw the mother of Christ and drew her in charcoal on the courthouse wall . . . When one is on the soil of one's ancestors, most anything can come to one . . . From force of habit, I suppose, I held Fern in my arms—that is, without at first noticing it. Then my mind came back to her. Her eyes, unusually weird and open, held me. Held God. He flowed in as I've seen the countryside flow in. Seen men. I must have done something—what, I dont know, in the confusion of my emotion. She sprang up. Rushed some distance from me. Fell to her knees, and began swaying, swaying. Her body was tortured with something it could not let out. Like boiling sap it flooded arms and fingers till she shook them as if they burned her. It found her throat, and spattered inarticulately in plaintive, convulsive sounds, mingled with calls to Christ Jesus. And then she sang, brokenly. A Jewish cantor singing with a broken voice. A child's voice, uncertain, or an old man's. Dusk hid her; I could hear only her song. It seemed to me as though she were pounding her head in anguish upon the ground. I rushed to her. She fainted in my arms.

There was talk about her fainting with me in the canefield. And I got one or two ugly looks from town men who'd set themselves up to protect her. In fact, there was talk of making me leave town. But they never did. They kept a watch-out for me, though. Shortly after, I came back North. From the train window I saw her as I crossed her road. Saw her on her porch, head tilted a little forward where the nail was, eyes vaguely focused on the sunset. Saw her face flow into them, the countryside and something that I call God, flow-ing into them . . . Nothing ever really happened. Nothing ever came to Fern, not even I. Something I would do for her. Some fine unnamed thing . . . And, friend, you? She is still living, I have reason to know. Her name, against the chance that you might happen down that way, is Fernie May Rosen.

NULLO[1]

A spray of pine-needles,
Dipped in western horizon gold,
Fell onto a path. .
Dry moulds of cow-hoofs. .
In the forest.
Rabbits knew not of their falling,
Nor did the forest catch aflame.

EVENING SONG

Full moon rising on the waters of my heart,
Lakes and moon and fires,
Cloine tires,
Holding her lips apart.

Promises of slumber leaving shore to charm the moon,
Miracle made vesper-keeps,
Cloine sleeps,
And I'll be sleeping soon.

Cloine, curled like the sleepy waters where the moon-waves
    start,
Radiant, resplendently she gleams,
Cloine dreams,
Lips pressed against my heart.

ESTHER

1

Nine.

Esther's hair falls in soft curls about her high-cheek-boned chalk-white face. Esther's hair would be beautiful if there were more gloss to it. And if her face were not prematurely serious, one would call it pretty. Her cheeks are too flat and dead for a girl of nine. Esther looks like a little white child, starched, frilled, as she walks slowly from her home towards her father's grocery store. She is about to turn in Broad from Maple Street. White and black men loafing on the corner hold no interest for her. Then a strange thing happens. A clean-muscled, magnificent, black-skinned Negro, whom she had heard her father mention as King Barlo, suddenly drops to his knees on a spot called the Spittoon. White men, unaware of him, continue squirting tobacco juice in his direction. The saffron fluid splashes on his face. His smooth black face begins to glisten and to shine. Soon, people notice him, and gather round. His eyes are rapturous upon the heavens. Lips and nostrils quiver. Barlo is in a religious trance. Town folks know it. They are not startled. They are not afraid. They gather round. Some beg boxes from the grocery stores.

From old McGregor's notion shop. A coffin-case is pressed
into use. Folks line the curb-stones. Business men close shop.
And Banker Warply parks his car close by. Silently, all await
the prophet's voice. The sheriff, a great florid fellow whose
leggings never meet around his bulging calves, swears in
three deputies. "Wall, y cant never tell what a nigger like
King Barlo might be up t." Soda bottles, five fingers full of
shine,[1] are passed to those who want them. A couple of stray
dogs start a fight. Old Goodlow's cow comes flopping up
the street. Barlo, still as an Indian fakir,[2] has not moved. The
town bell strikes six. The sun slips in behind a heavy mass of
horizon cloud. The crowd is hushed and expectant. Barlo's
under jaw relaxes, and his lips begin to move.

"Jesus has been awhisperin strange words deep down, O
way down deep, deep in my ears."

Hums of awe and of excitement.

"He called me to His side an said, 'Git down on your
knees beside me, son, Ise gwine t whisper in your ears.'"

An old sister cries, "Ah, Lord."

"'Ise agwine t whisper in your ears,' he said, an I replied,
'Thy will be done on earth as it is in heaven.'"

"Ah, Lord. Amen. Amen."

"An Lord Jesus whispered strange good words deep down,
O way down deep, deep in my ears. An He said, 'Tell em till
you feel your throat on fire.' I saw a vision. I saw a man
arise, an he was big an black an powerful—"

Some one yells, "Preach it, preacher, preach it!"

"—but his head was caught up in th clouds. An while he
was agazin at th heavens, heart filled up with th Lord, some
little white-ant biddies came an tied his feet to chains. They
led him t th coast, they led him t th sea, they led him across
th ocean an they didnt set him free. The old coast didnt miss
him, an th new coast wasnt free, he left the old-coast brothers,

t give birth t you an me. O Lord, great God Almighty, t give birth t you an me."

Barlo pauses. Old gray mothers are in tears. Fragments of melodies are being hummed. White folks are touched and curiously awed. Off to themselves, white and black preachers confer as to how best to rid themselves of the vagrant, usurping fellow. Barlo looks as though he is struggling to continue. People are hushed. One can hear weevils work. Dusk is falling rapidly, and the customary store lights fail to throw their feeble glow across the gray dust and flagging of the Georgia town. Barlo rises to his full height. He is immense. To the people he assumes the outlines of his visioned African. In a mighty voice he bellows:

"Brothers an sisters, turn your faces t th sweet face of the Lord, an fill your hearts with glory. Open your eyes an see th dawnin of th mornin light. Open your ears—"

Years afterwards Esther was told that at that very moment a great, heavy, rumbling voice actually was heard. That hosts of angels and of demons paraded up and down the streets all night. That King Barlo rode out of town astride a pitch-black bull that had a glowing gold ring in its nose. And that old Limp Underwood, who hated niggers, woke up next morning to find that he held a black man in his arms. This much is certain: an inspired Negress, of wide reputation for being sanctified, drew a portrait of a black madonna on the courthouse wall. And King Barlo left town. He left his image indelibly upon the mind of Esther. He became the starting point of the only living patterns that her mind was to know.

2

Sixteen.

Esther begins to dream. The low evening sun sets the windows of McGregor's notion shop aflame. Esther makes believe that they really are aflame. The town fire department rushes madly down the road. It ruthlessly shoves black and white idlers to one side. It whoops. It clangs. It rescues from the second-story window a dimpled infant which she claims for her own. How had she come by it? She thinks of it immaculately. It is a sin to think of it immaculately. She must dream no more. She must repent her sin. Another dream comes. There is no fire department. There are no heroic men. The fire starts. The loafers on the corner form a circle, chew their tobacco faster, and squirt juice just as fast as they can chew. Gallons on top of gallons they squirt upon the flames. The air reeks with the stench of scorched tobacco juice. Women, fat chunky Negro women, lean scrawny white women, pull their skirts up above their heads and display the most ludicrous underclothes. The women scoot in all directions from the danger zone. She alone is left to take the baby in her arms. But what a baby! Black, singed, woolly, tobacco-juice baby—ugly as sin. Once held to her breast, miraculous thing: its breath is sweet and its lips can nibble. She loves it frantically. Her joy in it changes the town folks' jeers to harmless jealousy, and she is left alone.

Twenty-two.

Esther's schooling is over. She works behind the counter of her father's grocery store. "To keep the money in the family," so he said. She is learning to make distinctions between the

business and the social worlds. "Good business comes from
remembering that the white folks dont divide the niggers, Esther. Be just as black as any man who has a silver dollar." Esther listlessly forgets that she is near white, and that her father
is the richest colored man in town. Black folk who drift in to
buy lard and snuff and flour of her, call her a sweet-natured,
accommodating girl. She learns their names. She forgets
them. She thinks about men. "I dont appeal to them. I wonder why." She recalls an affair she had with a little fair boy
while still in school. It had ended in her shame when he as
much as told her that for sweetness he preferred a lollipop.
She remembers the salesman from the North who wanted to
take her to the movies that first night he was in town. She refused, of course. And he never came back, having found out
who she was. She thinks of Barlo. Barlo's image gives her a
slightly stale thrill. She spices it by telling herself his glories.
Black. Magnetically so. Best cotton picker in the county, in
the state, in the whole world for that matter. Best man with
his fists, best man with dice, with a razor. Promoter of church
benefits. Of colored fairs. Vagrant preacher. Lover of all the
women for miles and miles around. Esther decides that she
loves him. And with a vague sense of life slipping by, she re-
solves that she will tell him so, whatever people say, the next
time he comes to town. After the making of this resolution
which becomes a sort of wedding cake for her to tuck beneath her pillow and go to sleep upon, she sees nothing of
Barlo for five years. Her hair thins. It looks like the dull silk
on puny corn ears. Her face pales until it is the color of the
gray dust that dances with dead cotton leaves. .

3

Esther is twenty-seven.

Esther sells lard and snuff and flour to vague black faces
that drift in her store to ask for them. Her eyes hardly see the
people to whom she gives change. Her body is lean and
beaten. She rests listlessly against the counter, too weary to
sit down. From the street some one shouts, "King Barlo has
come back to town." He passes her window, driving a large
new car. Cut-out open.[3] He veers to the curb, and steps out.
Barlo has made money on cotton during the war. He is as
rich as anyone. Esther suddenly is animate. She goes to her
door. She sees him at a distance, the center of a group of
credulous men. She hears the deep-bass rumble of his talk.
The sun swings low. McGregor's windows are aflame again.
Pale flame. A sharply dressed white girl passes by. For a moment Esther wishes that she might be like her. Not white; she
has no need for being that. But sharp, sporty, with get-up
about her. Barlo is connected with that wish. She mustnt
wish. Wishes only make you restless. Emptiness is a thing
that grows by being moved. "I'll not think. Not wish. Just
set my mind against it." Then the thought comes to her that
those purposeless, easy-going men will possess him, if she
doesnt. Purpose is not dead in her, now that she comes to
think of it. That loose women will have their arms around
him at Nat Bowle's place to-night. As if her veins are full of
fired sun-bleached southern shanties, a swift heat sweeps
them. Dead dreams, and a forgotten resolution are carried
upward by the flames. Pale flames. "They shant have him.
Oh, they shall not. Not if it kills me they shant have him."
Jerky, aflutter, she closes the store and starts home. Folks
lazing on store windowsills wonder what on earth can be the

matter with Jim Crane's gal, as she passes them. "Come to remember, she always was a little off, a little crazy, I reckon." Esther seeks her own room, and locks the door. Her mind is a pink meshbag filled with baby toes.

Using the noise of the town clock striking twelve to cover the creaks of her departure, Esther slips into the quiet road. The town, her parents, most everyone is sound asleep. This fact is a stable thing that comforts her. After sundown a chill wind came up from the west. It is still blowing, but to her it is a steady, settled thing like the cold. She wants her mind to be like that. Solid, contained, and blank as a sheet of darkened ice. She will not permit herself to notice the peculiar phosphorescent glitter of the sweet-gum leaves. Their movement would excite her. Exciting too, the recession of the dull familiar homes she knows so well. She doesnt know them at all. She closes her eyes, and holds them tightly. Wont do. Her being aware that they are closed recalls her purpose. She does not want to think of it. She opens them. She turns now into the deserted business street. The corrugated iron canopies and mule- and horse-gnawed hitching posts bring her a strange composure. Ghosts of the commonplaces of her daily life take stride with her and become her companions. And the echoes of her heels upon the flagging are rhythmically monotonous and soothing. Crossing the street at the corner of McGregor's notion shop, she thinks that the windows are a dull flame. Only a fancy. She walks faster. Then runs. A turn into a side street brings her abruptly to Nat Bowle's place. The house is squat and dark. It is always dark. Barlo is within. Quietly she opens the outside door and steps in. She passes through a small room. Pauses before a flight of stairs down which people's voices, muffled, come. The air is heavy with fresh tobacco smoke. It makes her sick. She wants to turn back. She goes up the steps. As if she were mounting to some great height, her head spins. She is violently dizzy. Blackness rushes to her eyes. And then she finds that she is in a large room. Barlo is before her.

"Well, I'm sholy damned—skuse me, but what, what brought you here, lil milk-white gal?"

"You." Her voice sounds like a frightened child's that calls homeward from some point miles away.

"Me?"

"Yes, you Barlo."

"This aint th place fer y. This aint th place fer y."

"I know. I know. But I've come for you."

"For me for what?"

She manages to look deep and straight into his eyes. He is slow at understanding. Guffaws and giggles break out from all around the room. A coarse woman's voice remarks, "So thats how th dictie niggers[4] does it." Laughs. "Mus give em credit fo their gall."

Esther doesnt hear. Barlo does. His faculties are jogged. She sees a smile, ugly and repulsive to her, working upward through thick licker fumes. Barlo seems hideous. The thought comes suddenly, that conception with a drunken man must be a mighty sin. She draws away, frozen. Like a somnambulist she wheels around and walks stiffly to the stairs. Down them. Jeers and hoots pelter bluntly upon her back. She steps out. There is no air, no street, and the town has completely disappeared.

CONVERSION

African Guardian of Souls,
Drunk with rum,
Feasting on a strange cassava,
Yielding to new words and a weak palabra
Of a white-faced sardonic god—
Grins, cries
Amen,
Shouts hosanna.

PORTRAIT IN GEORGIA

Hair—braided chestnut,
    coiled like a lyncher's rope,
Eyes—fagots,
Lips—old scars, or the first red blisters,
Breath—the last sweet scent of cane,
And her slim body, white as the ash
    of black flesh after flame.

BLOOD-BURNING MOON[1]

1

Up from the skeleton stone walls, up from the rotting floor boards and the solid hand-hewn beams of oak of the pre-war cotton factory,[2] dusk came. Up from the dusk the full moon came. Glowing like a fired pine-knot, it illumined the great door and soft showered the Negro shanties aligned along the single street of factory town. The full moon in the great door was an omen. Negro women improvised songs against its spell.

Louisa sang as she came over the crest of the hill from the white folks' kitchen. Her skin was the color of oak leaves on young trees in fall. Her breasts, firm and up-pointed like ripe acorns. And her singing had the low murmur of winds in fig trees. Bob Stone, younger son of the people she worked for, loved her. By the way the world reckons things, he had won her. By measure of that warm glow which came into her mind at thought of him, he had won her. Tom Burwell, whom the whole town called Big Boy, also loved her. But working in the fields all day, and far away from her, gave him no chance to show it. Though often enough of evenings he had tried to. Somehow, he never got along. Strong as he was with hands upon the ax or plow, he found it difficult to hold her. Or so he thought. But the fact was that he held her to factory town[3] more firmly than he thought for. His black balanced, and pulled against, the white of Stone, when she thought of them. And her mind was vaguely upon them as she came over the crest of the hill, coming from the white folks' kitchen. As she sang softly at the evil face of the full moon.

A strange stir was in her. Indolently, she tried to fix upon Bob or Tom as the cause of it. To meet Bob in the canebrake, as she was going to do an hour or so later, was nothing new. And Tom's proposal which she felt on its way to her could be indefinitely put off. Separately, there was no unusual significance to either one. But for some reason, they jumbled when her eyes gazed vacantly at the rising moon. And from the jumble came the stir that was strangely within her. Her lips trembled. The slow rhythm of her song grew agitant and restless. Rusty black and tan spotted hounds, lying in the dark corners of porches or prowling around back yards, put their noses in the air and caught its tremor. They began plaintively to yelp and howl. Chickens woke up and cackled. Intermittently, all over the countryside dogs barked and roosters crowed as if heralding a weird dawn or some ungodly awakening. The women sang lustily. Their songs were cotton-wads to stop their ears. Louisa came down into factory town and sank wearily upon the step before her home. The moon was rising towards a thick cloud-bank which soon would hide it.

> Red nigger moon. Sinner!
> Blood-burning moon. Sinner!
> Come out that fact'ry door.

2

Up from the deep dusk of a cleared spot on the edge of the forest a mellow glow arose and spread fan-wise into the low-hanging heavens. And all around the air was heavy with the scent of boiling cane. A large pile of cane-stalks lay like rib-boned shadows upon the ground. A mule, harnessed to a pole, trudged lazily round and round the pivot of the grinder. Beneath a swaying oil lamp, a Negro alternately whipped out at the mule, and fed cane-stalks to the grinder. A fat boy waddled pails of fresh ground juice between the grinder and the boiling stove. Steam came from the copper boiling pan. The scent of cane came from the copper pan and drenched the forest and the hill that sloped to factory town, beneath its fragrance. It drenched the men in circle seated around the stove. Some of them chewed at the white pulp of stalks, but there was no need for them to, if all they wanted was to taste the cane. One tasted it in factory town. And from factory town one could see the soft haze thrown by the glowing stove upon the low-hanging heavens.

Old David Georgia stirred the thickening syrup with a long ladle, and ever so often drew it off. Old David Georgia tended his stove and told tales about the white folks, about moonshining and cotton picking, and about sweet nigger gals, to the men who sat there about his stove to listen to him. Tom Burwell chewed cane-stalk and laughed with the others till someone mentioned Louisa. Till some one said something about Louisa and Bob Stone, about the silk stockings she must have gotten from him. Blood ran up Tom's neck hotter than the glow that flooded from the stove. He sprang up. Glared at the men and said, "She's my gal." Will Manning laughed. Tom strode over to him. Yanked him up and knocked him to the ground. Several of Manning's friends got up to fight for him. Tom whipped out a long knife and would have cut them to shreds if they hadnt ducked into the woods. Tom had had enough. He nodded to Old David Georgia and swung down the path to factory town. Just then, the dogs started barking and the roosters began to crow. Tom felt funny. Away from the fight, away from the stove, chill got to him. He shivered. He shuddered when he saw the full moon rising towards the cloud-bank. He who didnt give a godam for the fears of old women. He forced his mind to fasten on Louisa. Bob Stone. Better not be. He turned into the street and saw Louisa sitting before her home. He went towards her, ambling, touched the brim of a marvelously shaped, spotted, felt hat, said he wanted to say something to her, and then found that he didnt know what he had to say, or if he did, that he couldnt say it. He shoved his big fists in his overalls, grinned, and started to move off.

"Youall want me, Tom?"

"Thats what us wants, sho, Louisa."

"Well, here I am—"

"An here I is, but that aint ahelpin none, all th same."

"You wanted to say something? . ."

"I did that, sho. But words is like th spots on dice: no matter how y fumbles em, there's times when they jes wont come. I dunno why. Seems like th love I feels fo yo done stole m tongue. I got it now. Whee! Louisa, honey, I oughtnt tell y, I feel I oughtnt cause yo is young an goes t church an I has had other gals, but Louisa I sho do love y. Lil gal, Ise watched y from them first days when youall sat right here befo yo door befo th well an sang sometimes in a way that like t broke m heart. Ise carried y with me into th fields, day after day, an after that, an I sho can plow when yo is there, an I can pick cotton. Yassur! Come near beatin Barlo yesterday. I sho did. Yassur! An next year if ole Stone'll trust me, I'll have a farm. My own. My bales will buy yo what y gets from white folks now. Silk stockings an purple dresses—course I dont believe what some folks been whisperin as t how y gets them things now. White folks always did do for niggers what they likes. An they jes cant help alikin yo, Louisa. Bob Stone likes y. Course he does. But not th way folks is awhisperin. Does he, hon?"

"I dont know what you mean, Tom."

"Course y dont. Ise already cut two niggers. Had t hon, t tell em so. Niggers always tryin t make somethin out a nothin. An then besides, white folks aint up t them tricks so much nowadays. Godam better not be. Leastawise not with yo. Cause I wouldnt stand f it. Nassur."

"What would you do, Tom?"

"Cut him jes like I cut a nigger."

"No, Tom—"

"I said I would an there aint no mo to it. But that aint th talk f now. Sing, honey Louisa, an while I'm listenin t y I'll be makin love."

Tom took her hand in his. Against the tough thickness of his own, hers felt soft and small. His huge body slipped down to the step beside her. The full moon sank upward into the deep purple of the cloud-bank. An old woman brought a lighted lamp and hung it on the common well whose bulky shadow squatted in the middle of the road, opposite Tom and Louisa. The old woman lifted the well-lid, took hold the chain, and began drawing up the heavy bucket. As she did so, she sang. Figures shifted, restless-like, between lamp and window in the front rooms of the shanties. Shadows of the figures fought each other on the gray dust of the road. Figures raised the windows and joined the old woman in song. Louisa and Tom, the whole street, singing:

Red nigger moon. Sinner!
Blood-burning moon. Sinner!
Come out that fact'ry door.

3

Bob Stone sauntered from his veranda out into the gloom of
fir trees and magnolias. The clear white of his skin paled,
and the flush of his cheeks turned purple. As if to balance
this outer change, his mind became consciously a white
man's. He passed the house with its huge open hearth which,
in the days of slavery, was the plantation cookery. He saw
Louisa bent over that hearth. He went in as a master should
and took her. Direct, honest, bold. None of this sneaking
that he had to go through now. The contrast was repulsive to
him. His family had lost ground. Hell no, his family still
owned the niggers, practically. Damned if they did, or he
wouldnt have to duck around so. What would they think
if they knew? His mother? His sister? He shouldnt mention
them, shouldnt think of them in this connection. There in
the dusk he blushed at doing so. Fellows about town were all
right, but how about his friends up North? He could see
them incredible, repulsed. They didnt know. The thought
first made him laugh. Then, with their eyes still upon him,
he began to feel embarrassed. He felt the need of explaining
things to them. Explain hell. They wouldnt understand, and
moreover, who ever heard of a Southerner getting on his
knees to any Yankee, or anyone. No sir. He was going to see
Louisa to-night, and love her. She was lovely—in her way.
Nigger way. What way was that? Damned if he knew. Must
know. He'd known her long enough to know. Was there
something about niggers that you couldnt know? Listening

to them at church didnt tell you anything. Looking at them didnt tell you anything. Talking to them didnt tell you anything—unless it was gossip, unless they wanted to talk. Of course, about farming, and licker, and craps[4]—but those werent nigger. Nigger was something more. How much more? Something to be afraid of, more? Hell no. Who ever heard of being afraid of a nigger? Tom Burwell. Cartwell had told him that Tom went with Louisa after she reached home. No sir. No nigger had ever been with his girl. He'd like to see one try. Some position for him to be in. Him, Bob Stone, of the old Stone family, in a scrap with a nigger over a nigger girl. In the good old days . . . Ha! Those were the days. His family had lost ground. Not so much, though. Enough for him to have to cut through old Lemon's canefield by way of the woods, that he might meet her. She was worth it. Beautiful nigger gal. Why nigger? Why not, just gal? No, it was because she was nigger that he went to her. Sweet . . . The scent of boiling cane came to him. Then he saw the rich glow of the stove. He heard the voices of the men circled around it. He was about to skirt the clearing when he heard his own name mentioned. He stopped. Quivering. Leaning against a tree, he listened.

"Bad nigger. Yassur, he sho is one bad nigger when he gets started."

"Tom Burwell's been on th gang[5] three times fo cuttin men."

"What y think he's agwine t do t Bob Stone?"

"Dunno yet. He aint found out. When he does—Baby!"

"Aint no tellin."

"Young Stone aint no quitter an I ken tell y that. Blood of th old uns in his veins."

"Thats right. He'll scrap, sho."

"Be gettin too hot f niggers round this away."

"Shut up, nigger. Y dont know what y talkin bout."

Bob Stone's ears burned as though he had been holding them over the stove. Sizzling heat welled up within him. His feet felt as if they rested on red-hot coals. They stung him to quick movement. He circled the fringe of the glowing. Not a twig cracked beneath his feet. He reached the path that led to factory town. Plunged furiously down it. Halfway along, a blindness within him veered him aside. He crashed into the bordering canebrake. Cane leaves cut his face and lips. He tasted blood. He threw himself down and dug his fingers in the ground. The earth was cool. Cane-roots took the fever from his hands. After a long while, or so it seemed to him, the thought came to him that it must be time to see Louisa. He got to his feet and walked calmly to their meeting place. No Louisa. Tom Burwell had her. Veins in his forehead bulged and distended. Saliva moistened the dried blood on his lips. He bit down on his lips. He tasted blood. Not his own blood; Tom Burwell's blood. Bob drove through the cane and out again upon the road. A hound swung down the path before him towards factory town. Bob couldnt see it. The dog loped aside to let him pass. Bob's blind rushing made him stumble over it. He fell with a thud that dazed him. The hound yelped. Answering yelps came from all over the countryside. Chickens cackled. Roosters crowed, heralding the bloodshot eyes of southern awakening. Singers in the town were silenced. They shut their windows down. Palpitant between the rooster crows, a chill hush settled upon the huddled forms of Tom and Louisa. A figure rushed from the shadow and stood before them. Tom popped to his feet.

"Whats y want?"

"I'm Bob Stone."

"Yassur—an I'm Tom Burwell. Whats y want?"

Bob lunged at him. Tom side-stepped, caught him by the shoulder, and flung him to the ground. Straddled him.

"Let me up."

"Yassur—but watch yo doins, Bob Stone."

A few dark figures, drawn by the sound of scuffle, stood about them. Bob sprang to his feet.

"Fight like a man, Tom Burwell, an I'll lick y."

Again he lunged. Tom side-stepped and flung him to the ground. Straddled him.

"Get off me, you godam nigger you."

"Yo sho has started somethin now. Get up."

Tom yanked him up and began hammering at him. Each blow sounded as if it smashed into a precious, irreplaceable soft something. Beneath them, Bob staggered back. He reached in his pocket and whipped out a knife.

"Thats my game, sho."

Blue flash, a steel blade slashed across Bob Stone's throat. He had a sweetish sick feeling. Blood began to flow. Then he felt a sharp twitch of pain. He let his knife drop. He slapped one hand against his neck. He pressed the other on top of his head as if to hold it down. He groaned. He turned, and staggered towards the crest of the hill in the direction of white town. Negroes who had seen the fight slunk into their homes and blew the lamps out. Louisa, dazed, hysterical, refused to go indoors. She slipped, crumbled, her body loosely propped against the woodwork of the well. Tom Burwell leaned against it. He seemed rooted there.

Bob reached Broad Street. White men rushed up to him. He collapsed in their arms.

"Tom Burwell. . . ."

White men like ants upon a forage rushed about. Except for the taut hum of their moving, all was silent. Shotguns,

revolvers, rope, kerosene, torches. Two high-powered cars
with glaring search-lights. They came together. The taut
hum rose to a low roar. Then nothing could be heard but the
flop of their feet in the thick dust of the road. The moving
body of their silence preceded them over the crest of the hill
into factory town. It flattened the Negroes beneath it. It
rolled to the wall of the factory, where it stopped. Tom knew
that they were coming. He couldnt move. And then he saw
the search-lights of the two cars glaring down on him. A
quick shock went through him. He stiffened. He started to
run. A yell went up from the mob. Tom wheeled about and
faced them. They poured down on him. They swarmed. A
large man with dead-white face and flabby cheeks came to
him and almost jabbed a gun-barrel through his guts.

"Hands behind y, nigger."

Tom's wrists were bound. The big man shoved him to the
well. Burn him over it, and when the woodwork caved in, his
body would drop to the bottom. Two deaths for a godam nigger. Louisa was driven back. The mob pushed in. Its pressure,
its momentum was too great. Drag him to the factory. Wood
and stakes already there. Tom moved in the direction indi-
cated. But they had to drag him. They reached the great door.
Too many to get in there. The mob divided and flowed around
the walls to either side. The big man shoved him through the
door. The mob pressed in from the sides. Taut humming. No
words. A stake was sunk into the ground. Rotting floor
boards piled around it. Kerosene poured on the rotting floor
boards. Tom bound to the stake. His breast was bare. Nails
scratches let little lines of blood trickle down and mat into
the hair. His face, his eyes were set and stony. Except for irregular breathing, one would have thought him already dead.
Torches were flung onto the pile. A great flare muffled in black
smoke shot upward. The mob yelled. The mob was silent. Now

Tom could be seen within the flames. Only his head, erect. lean, like a blackened stone. Stench of burning flesh soaked the air. Tom's eyes popped. His head settled downward. The mob yelled. Its yell echoed against the skeleton stone walls and sounded like a hundred yells. Like a hundred mobs yelling. Its yell thudded against the thick front wall and fell back. Ghost of a yell slipped through the flames and out the great door of the factory. It fluttered like a dying thing down the single street of factory town. Louisa, upon the step before her home, did not hear it, but her eyes opened slowly. They saw the full moon glowing in the great door. The full moon, an evil thing, an omen, soft showering the homes of folks she knew. Where were they, these people? She'd sing, and perhaps they'd come out and join her. Perhaps Tom Burwell would come. At any rate, the full moon in the great door was an omen which she must sing to:

> Red nigger moon. Sinner!
> Blood-burning moon. Sinner!
> Come out that fact'ry door.

SEVENTH STREET[1]

Money burns the pocket, pocket hurts,
Bootleggers[2] in silken shirts,
Ballooned, zooming Cadillacs,
Whizzing, whizzing down the street-car tracks.

Seventh Street is a bastard of Prohibition[3] and the War. A crude-boned, soft-skinned wedge of nigger life breathing its loafer air, jazz songs and love, thrusting unconscious rhythms, black reddish blood into the white and white-washed wood of Washington. Stale soggy wood of Washington. Wedges rust in soggy wood . . . Split it! In two! Again! Shred it! . . the sun. Wedges are brilliant in the sun; ribbons of wet wood dry and blow away. Black reddish blood. Pouring for crude-boned soft-skinned life, who set you flowing? Blood suckers of the War would spin in a frenzy of dizziness if they drank your blood. Prohibition would put a stop to it. Who set you flowing? White and whitewash disappear in blood. Who set you flowing? Flowing down the smooth asphalt of Seventh Street, in shanties, brick office buildings, theaters, drug stores, restaurants, and cabarets? Eddying on the corners? Swirling like a blood-red smoke up where the buzzards fly in heaven? God would not dare to suck black

red blood. A Nigger God! He would duck his head in shame
and call for the Judgment Day. Who set you flowing?

> Money burns the pocket, pocket hurts,
> Bootleggers in silken shirts,
> Ballooned, zooming Cadillacs,
> Whizzing, whizzing down the street-car tracks.

RHOBERT

Rhobert wears a house, like a monstrous diver's helmet, on his head. His legs are banty-bowed and shaky because as a child he had rickets. He is way down. Rods of the house like antennæ of a dead thing, stuffed, prop up in the air. He is way down. He is sinking. His house is a dead thing that weights him down. He is sinking as a diver would sink in mud should the water be drawn off. Life is a murky, wiggling, microscopic water that compresses him. Compresses his helmet and would crush it the minute that he pulled his head out. He has to keep it in. Life is water that is being drawn off.

Brother, life is water that is being drawn off.
Brother, life is water that is being drawn off.

The dead house is stuffed. The stuffing is alive. It is sinful to draw one's head out of live stuffing in a dead house. The propped-up antennæ would cave in and the stuffing be strewn . . shredded life-pulp . . in the water. It is sinful to have one's own head crushed. Rhobert is an upright man whose legs are banty-bowed and shaky because as a child he had rickets. The earth is round. Heaven is a sphere that surrounds it. Sink where you will. God is a Red Cross man with a dredge and a respiration-pump who's waiting for you at the opposite periphery. God built the house. He blew His breath into its stuffing. It is good to to die obeying Him who can do these things.

A futile something like the dead house wraps the live stuffing of the question: how long before the water will be drawn off? Rhobert does not care. Like most men who wear monstrous helmets, the pressure it exerts is enough to convince him of its practical infinity. And he cares not two straws as to whether or not he will ever see his wife and children again. Many a time he's seen them drown in his dreams and has kicked about joyously in the mud for days after. One thing about him goes straight to the heart. He has an Adam's-apple which strains sometimes as if he were painfully gulping great globules of air . . air floating shredded life-pulp. It is a sad thing to see a banty-bowed, shaky, ricket-legged man straining the raw insides of his throat against smooth air. Holding furtive thoughts about the glory of pulp-heads strewn in water. . He is way down. Down. Mud, coming to his banty knees, almost hides them. Soon people will be looking at him and calling him a strong man. No doubt he is for one who has had rickets. Lets give it to him. Lets call him great when the water shall have been all drawn off. Lets build a monument and set it in the ooze where he goes down. A monument of hewn oak, carved in nigger-heads. Lets open our throats, brother, and sing "Deep River"[1] when he goes down.

> Brother, Rhobert is sinking.
> Lets open our throats, brother,
> Lets sing Deep River when he goes down.

AVEY

For a long while she was nothing more to me than one of those skirted beings whom boys at a certain age disdain to play with. Just how I came to love her, timidly, and with secret blushes, I do not know. But that I did was brought home to me one night, the first night that Ned wore his long pants. Us fellers were seated on the curb before an apartment house where she had gone in. The young trees had not outgrown their boxes then. V Street[1] was lined with them. When our legs grew cramped and stiff from the cold of the stone, we'd stand around a box and whittle it. I like to think now that there was a hidden purpose in the way we hacked them with our knives. I like to feel that something deep in me responded to the trees, the young trees that whinnied like colts impatient to be let free . . . On the particular night I have in mind, we were waiting for the top-floor light to go out. We wanted to see Avey leave the flat. This night she stayed longer than usual and gave us a chance to complete the plans of how we were going to stone and beat that feller on the top floor out of town. Ned especially had it in for him. He was about to throw a brick up at the window when at last the room went dark. Some minutes passed. Then Avey, as unconcerned as if she had been paying an old-maid aunt a visit, came out. I don't remember what she had on, and all that sort of thing.

But I do know that I turned hot as bare pavements in the summertime at Ned's boast: "Hell, bet I could get her too if you little niggers weren't always spying and crabbing everything." I didnt say a word to him. It wasnt my way then. I just stood there like the others, and something like a fuse burned up inside of me. She never noticed us, but swung along lazy and easy as anything. We sauntered to the corner and watched her till her door banged to. Ned repeated what he'd said. I didnt seem to care. Sitting around old Mush-Head's bread box, the discussion began. "Hang if I can see how she gets away with it," Doc started. Ned knew, of course. There was nothing he didnt know when it came to women. He dilated on the emotional needs of girls. Said they werent much different from men in that respect. And concluded with the solemn avowal: "It does em good." None of us liked Ned much. We all talked dirt; but it was the way he said it. And then too, a couple of the fellers had sisters and had caught Ned playing with them. But there was no disputing the superiority of his smutty wisdom. Bubs Sanborn, whose mother was friendly with Avey's, had overheard the old ladies talking. "Avey's mother's ont her," he said. We thought that only natural and began to guess at what would happen. Some one said she'd marry that feller on the top floor. Ned called that a lie because Avey was going to marry nobody but him. We had our doubts about that, but we did agree that she'd soon leave school and marry some one. The gang broke up, and I went home, picturing myself as married.

Nothing I did seemed able to change Avey's indifference to me. I played basket-ball, and when I'd make a long clean shot she'd clap with the others, louder than they, I thought. I'd meet her on the street, and there'd be no difference in the way she said hello. She never took the trouble to call me by

my name. On the days for drill, I'd let my voice down a tone
and call for a complicated maneuver when I saw her coming.
She'd smile appreciation, but it was an impersonal smile,
never for me. It was on a summer excursion down to River-
view that she first seemed to take me into account. The day
had been spent riding merry-go-rounds, scenic-railways, and
shoot-the-chutes. We had been in swimming and we had
danced. I was a crack swimmer then. She didnt know how. I
held her up and showed her how to kick her legs and draw
her arms. Of course she didnt learn in one day, but she
thanked me for bothering with her. I was also somewhat of a
dancer. And I had already noticed that love can start on a
dance floor. We danced. But though I held her tightly in my
arms, she was way away. That college feller who lived on the
top floor was somewhere making money for the next year. I
imagined that she was thinking, wishing for him. Ned was
along. He treated her until his money gave out. She went
with another feller. Ned got sore. One by one the boys'
money gave out. She left them. And they got sore. Every one
of them but me got sore. This is the reason, I guess, why I
had her to myself on the top deck of the *Jane Mosely* that
night as we puffed up the Potomac, coming home. The moon
was brilliant. The air was sweet like clover. And every now
and then, a salt tang, a stale drift of sea-weed. It was not my
mind's fault if it went romancing. I should have taken her in
my arms the minute we were stowed in that old lifeboat. I
dallied, dreaming. She took me in hers. And I could feel by
the touch of it that it wasnt a man-to-woman love. It made
me restless. I felt chagrined. I didnt know what it was, but I
did know that I couldnt handle it. She ran her fingers through
my hair and kissed my forehead. I itched to break through
her tenderness to passion. I wanted her to take me in her
arms as I knew she had that college feller. I wanted her to

love me passionately as she did him. I gave her one burning
kiss. Then she laid me in her lap as if I were a child. Helpless.
I got sore when she started to hum a lullaby. She wouldnt let
me go. I talked. I knew damned well that I could beat her at
that. Her eyes were soft and misty, the curves of her lips
were wistful, and her smile seemed indulgent of the irrele-
vance of my remarks. I gave up at last and let her love me,
silently, in her own way. The moon was brilliant. The air
was sweet like clover, and every now and then, a salt tang, a
stale drift of sea-weed . . .

The next time I came close to her was the following summer at Harpers Ferry.[2] We were sitting on a flat projecting
rock they give the name of Lover's Leap. Some one is supposed to have jumped off it. The river is about six hundred
feet beneath. A railroad track runs up the valley and curves
out of sight where part of the mountain rock had to be
blasted away to make room for it. The engines of this valley
have a whistle, the echoes of which sound like iterated gasps
and sobs. I always think of them as crude music from the
soul of Avey. We sat there holding hands. Our palms were
soft and warm against each other. Our fingers were not tight.
She would not let them be. She would not let me twist them.
I wanted to talk. To explain what I meant to her. Avey was as
silent as those great trees whose tops we looked down upon.
She has always been like that. At least, to me. I had the notion that if I really wanted to, I could do with her just what I
pleased. Like one can strip a tree. I did kiss her. I even let my
hands cup her breasts. When I was through, she'd seek my
hand and hold it till my pulse cooled down. Evening after
evening we sat there. I tried to get her to talk about that college feller. She never would. There was no set time to go
home. None of my family had come down. And as for hers,

she didnt give a hang about them. The general gossips could hardly say more than they had. The boarding-house porch was always deserted when we returned. No one saw us enter, so the time was set conveniently for scandal. This worried me a little, for I thought it might keep Avey from getting an appointment in the schools. She didnt care. She had finished normal school.[3] They could give her a job if they wanted to. As time went on, her indifference to things began to pique me; I was ambitious. I left the Ferry earlier than she did. I was going off to college. The more I thought of it, the more I resented, yes, hell, thats what it was, her downright laziness. Sloppy indolence. There was no excuse for a healthy girl taking life so easy. Hell! she was no better than a cow. I was certain that she was a cow when I felt an udder in a Wisconsin stock-judging class. Among those energetic Swedes, or whatever they are, I decided to forget her. For two years I thought I did. When I'd come home for the summer she'd be away. And before she returned, I'd be gone. We never wrote; she was too damned lazy for that. But what a bluff I put up about forgetting her. The girls up that way, at least the ones I knew, havent got the stuff: they dont know how to love. Giving themselves completely was tame beside just the holding of Avey's hand. One day I received a note from her. The writing, I decided, was slovenly. She wrote on a torn bit of notebook paper. The envelope had a faint perfume that I remembered. A single line told me she had lost her school and was going away. I comforted myself with the reflection that shame held no pain for one so indolent as she. Nevertheless, I left Wisconsin that year for good. Washington had seemingly forgotten her. I hunted Ned. Between curses, I caught his opinion of her. She was no better than a whore. I saw her mother on the street. The same old pinchbeck, jerky-gaited creature that I'd always known.

Perhaps five years passed. The business of hunting a job or something or other had bruised my vanity so that I could recognize it. I felt old. Avey and my real relation to her, I thought I came to know. I wanted to see her. I had been told that she was in New York. As I had no money, I hiked and bummed my way there. I got work in a ship-yard and walked the streets at night, hoping to meet her. Failing in this, I saved enough to pay my fare back home. One evening in early June, just at the time when dusk is most lovely on the eastern horizon, I saw Avey, indolent as ever, leaning on the arm of a man, strolling under the recently lit arc-lights of U Street.⁴ She had almost passed before she recognized me. She showed no surprise. The puff over her eyes had grown heavier. The eyes themselves were still sleepy-large, and beautiful. I had almost concluded—indifferent. "You look older," was what she said. I wanted to convince her that I was, so I asked her to walk with me. The man whom she was with, and whom she never took the trouble to introduce, at a nod from her, hailed a taxi, and drove away. That gave me a notion of what she had been used to. Her dress was of some fine, costly stuff. I suggested the park, and then added that the grass might stain her skirt. Let it get stained, she said, for where it came from there are others.

I have a spot in Soldier's Home⁵ to which I always go when I want the simple beauty of another's soul. Robins spring about the lawn all day. They leave their footprints in the grass. I imagine that the grass at night smells sweet and fresh because of them. The ground is high. Washington lies below. Its light spreads like a blush against the darkened sky. Against the soft dusk sky of Washington. And when the wind is from the South, soil of my homeland falls like a fertile shower upon the lean streets of the city. Upon my hill in

Soldier's Home. I know the policeman who watches the place of nights. When I go there alone, I talk to him. I tell him I come there to find the truth that people bury in their hearts. I tell him that I do not come there with a girl to do the thing he's paid to watch out for. I look deep in his eyes when I say these things, and he believes me. He comes over to see who it is on the grass. I say hello to him. He greets me in the same way and goes off searching for other black splotches upon the lawn. Avey and I went there. A band in one of the buildings a fair distance off was playing a march. I wished they would stop. Their playing was like a tin spoon in one's mouth. I wanted the Howard Glee Club[6] to sing "Deep River,"[7] from the road. To sing "Deep River, Deep River," from the road . . . Other than the first comments, Avey had been silent. I started to hum a folk-tune. She slipped her hand in mine. Pillowed her head as best she could upon my arm. Kissed the hand that she was holding and listened, or so I thought, to what I had to say. I traced my development from the early days up to the present time, the phase in which I could understand her. I described her own nature and temperament. Told how they needed a larger life for their expression. How incapable Washington was of understanding that need. How it could not meet it. I pointed out that in lieu of proper channels, her emotions had overflowed into paths that dissipated them. I talked, beautifully I thought, about an art that would be born, an art that would open the way for women the likes of her. I asked her to hope, and build up an inner life against the coming of that day. I recited some of my own things to her. I sang, with a strange quiver in my voice, a promise-song. And then I began to wonder why her hand had not once returned a single pressure. My old-time feeling about her laziness came back. I spoke sharply. My policeman friend passed by. I said hello to him. As he went away, I began to visualize certain possibilities. An immediate and urgent passion swept over me. Then I looked at Avey. Her heavy eyes were closed. Her breathing was as faint and regular as a child's in slumber. My passion died. I was afraid to move lest I disturb her. Hours and hours, I guess it was, she lay there. My body grew numb. I shivered. I coughed. I wanted to get up and whittle at the boxes of young trees. I withdrew my hand. I raised her head to waken her. She did not stir. I got up and walked around. I found my policeman friend and talked to him. We both came up, and bent over her. He said it would be all right for her to stay there just so long as she got away before the workmen came at dawn. A blanket was borrowed from a neighbor house. I sat beside her through the night. I saw the dawn steal over Washington. The Capitol dome looked like a gray ghost ship drifting in from sea. Avey's face was pale, and her eyes were heavy. She did not have the gray crimson-splashed beauty of the dawn. I hated to wake her. Orphan-woman . . .

BEEHIVE

Within this black hive to-night
There swarm a million bees;
Bees passing in and out the moon,
Bees escaping out the moon,
Bees returning through the moon,
Silver bees intently buzzing,
Silver honey dripping from the swarm of bees
Earth is a waxen cell of the world comb,
And I, a drone,
Lying on my back,
Lipping honey,
Getting drunk with silver honey,
Wish that I might fly out past the moon
And curl forever in some far-off farmyard flower.

STORM ENDING

Thunder blossoms gorgeously above our heads.
Great, hollow, bell-like flowers,
Rumbling in the wind,
Stretching clappers to strike our ears . .
Full-lipped flowers
Bitten by the sun
Bleeding rain
Dripping rain like golden honey—
And the sweet earth flying from the thunder.

THEATER

Life of nigger alleys, of pool rooms and restaurants and near-beer saloons[1] soaks into the walls of Howard Theater[2] and sets them throbbing jazz songs. Black-skinned, they dance and shout above the tick and trill of white-walled buildings. At night, they open doors to people who come in to stamp their feet and shout. At night, road-shows volley songs into the mass-heart of black people. Songs soak the walls and seep out to the nigger life of alleys and near-beer saloons, of the Poodle Dog and Black Bear cabarets. Afternoons, the house is dark, and the walls are sleeping singers until rehearsal begins. Or until John comes within them. Then they start throbbing to a subtle syncopation. And the space-dark air grows softly luminous.

John is the manager's brother. He is seated at the center of the theater, just before rehearsal. Light streaks down upon him from a window high above. One half his face is orange in it. One half his face is in shadow. The soft glow of the house rushes to, and compacts about, the shaft of light. John's mind coincides with the shaft of light. Thoughts rush to, and compact about it. Life of the house and of the slowly awakening stage swirls to the body of John, and thrills it. John's body is separate from the thoughts that pack his mind.

Stage-lights, soft, as if they shine through clear pink fingers.

Beneath them, hid by the shadow of a set, Dorris. Other chorus girls drift in. John feels them in the mass. And as if his own body were the mass-heart of a black audience listening to them singing, he wants to stamp his feet and shout. His mind, contained above desires of his body, singles the girls out, and tries to trace origins and plot destinies.

A pianist slips into the pit and improvises jazz. The walls awake. Arms of the girls, and their limbs, which . . jazz, jazz . . by lifting up their tight street skirts they set free, jab the air and clog the floor in rhythm to the music. (Lift your skirts, Baby, and talk t papa!) Crude, individualized, and yet . . monotonous . . .

John: Soon the director will herd you, my full-lipped, distant beauties, and tame you, and blunt your sharp thrusts in loosely suggestive movements, appropriate to Broadway. (O dance!) Soon the audience will paint your dusk faces white, and call you beautiful. (O dance!) Soon I . . . (O dance!) I'd like . . .

Girls laugh and shout. Sing discordant snatches of other jazz songs. Whirl with loose passion into the arms of passing show-men.

John: Too thick. Too easy. Too monotonous. Her whom I'd love I'd leave before she knew that I was with her. Her? Which? (O dance!) I'd like to . . .

Girls dance and sing. Men clap. The walls sing and press inward. They press the men and girls, they press John towards a center of physical ecstasy. Go to it, Baby! Fan yourself, and feed your papa! Put . . nobody lied . . and take[3] . . when they said I cried over you. No lie! The glitter and color of stacked scenes, the gilt and brass and crimson of the house, converge towards a center of physical ecstasy. John's feet and torso and his blood press in. He wills thought to rid his mind of passion.

"All right, girls. Alaska. Miss Reynolds, please."

The director wants to get the rehearsal through with.

The girls line up. John sees the front row: dancing ponies. The rest are in shadow. The leading lady fits loosely in the front. Lack-life, monotonous. "One, two, three—" Music starts. The song is somewhere where it will not strain the leading lady's throat. The dance is somewhere where it will not strain the girls. Above the staleness, one dancer throws herself into it. Dorris. John sees her. Her hair, crisp-curled, is bobbed.[4] Bushy, black hair bobbing about her lemon-colored face. Her lips are curiously full, and very red. Her limbs in silk purple stockings are lovely. John feels them. Desires her. Holds off.

John: Stage-door johnny;[5] chorus-girl. No, that would be all right. Dictie,[6] educated, stuck-up; show-girl. Yep. Her suspicion would be stronger than her passion. It wouldnt work. Keep her loveliness. Let her go.

Dorris sees John and knows that he is looking at her. Her own glowing is too rich a thing to let her feel the slimness of his diluted passion.

"Who's that?" she asks her dancing partner.

"Th manager's brother. Dictie. Nothin doin, hon."

Dorris tosses her head and dances for him until she feels she has him. Then, withdrawing disdainfully, she flirts with the director.

Dorris: Nothin doin? How come? Aint I as good as him? Couldnt I have got an education if I'd wanted one? Dont I know respectable folks, lots of em, in Philadelphia and New York and Chicago? Aint I had men as good as him? Better. Doctors an lawyers. Whats a manager's brother, anyhow?

Two steps back, and two steps front.

"Say, Mame, where do you get that stuff?"

"Whatshmean, Dorris?"

"If you two girls cant listen to what I'm telling you, I know where I can get some who can. Now listen."

Mame: Go to hell, you black bastard.

Dorris: Whats eatin at him, anyway?

"Now follow me in this, you girls. Its three counts to the right, three counts to the left, and then you shimmy—"[7]

John:—and then you shimmy. I'll bet she can. Some good cabaret, with rooms upstairs. And what in hell do you think you'd get from it? Youre going wrong. Here's right: get her to herself—(Christ, but how she'd bore you after the first five minutes)—not if you get her right she wouldnt. Touch her, I mean. To herself—in some room perhaps. Some cheap, dingy bedroom. Hell no. Cant be done. But the point is, brother John, it can be done. Get her to herself somewhere, any-where. Go down in yourself—and she'd be calling you all sorts of asses while you were in the process of going down. Hold em, bud. Cant be done. Let her go. (Dance and I'll love you!) And keep her loveliness.

"All right now, Chicken Chaser.[8] Dorris and girls. Where's Dorris? I told you to stay on the stage, didnt I? Well? Now thats enough. All right. All right there, Professor?[9] All right. One, two, three—"

Dorris swings to the front. The line of girls, four deep, blurs within the shadow of suspended scenes. Dorris wants to dance. The director feels that and steps to one side. He smiles, and picks her for a leading lady, one of these days. Odd ends of stage-men emerge from the wings, and stare and clap. A crap game in the alley suddenly ends. Black faces crowd the rear stage doors. The girls, catching joy from Dor-ris, whip up within the footlights' glow. They forget set steps; they find their own. The director forgets to bawl them out. Dorris dances.

John: Her head bobs to Broadway. Dance from yourself. Dance! O just a little more.

Dorris' eyes burn across the space of seats to him.

Dorris: I bet he can love. Hell, he cant love. He's too skinny. His lips are too skinny. He wouldnt love me anyway, only for that. But I'd get a pair of silk stockings out of it. Red silk. I got purple. Cut it, kid. You cant win him to respect you that away. He wouldnt anyway. Maybe he would. Maybe he'd love. I've heard em say that men who look like him (what does he look like?) will marry if they love. O will you love me? And give me kids, and a home, and everything? (I'd like to make your nest, and honest, hon, I wouldnt run out on you.) You will if I make you. Just watch me.

Dorris dances. She forgets her tricks. She dances.

Glorious songs are the muscles of her limbs.

And her singing is of canebrake loves and mangrove feastings.

The walls press in, singing. Flesh of a throbbing body, they press close to John and Dorris. They close them in. John's heart beats tensely against her dancing body. Walls press his mind within his heart. And then, the shaft of light goes out the window high above him. John's mind sweeps up to follow it. Mind pulls him upward into dream.

Dorris dances . . .

John dreams:

Dorris is dressed in a loose black gown splashed with lemon ribbons. Her feet taper long and slim from trim ankles. She waits for him just inside the stage door. John, collar and tie colorful and flaring, walks towards the stage door. There are no trees in the alley. But his feet feel as though they step on autumn leaves whose rustle has been pressed out of them by the passing of a million satin slippers. The air is sweet with roasting chestnuts, sweet with bonfires of old leaves. John's melancholy is a deep thing that seals all senses but his eyes, and makes him whole.

Dorris knows that he is coming. Just at the right moment she steps from the door, as if there were no door. Her face is tinted like the autumn alley. Of old flowers, or of a southern canefield, her perfume. "Glorious Dorris." So his eyes speak. And their sadness is too deep for sweet untruth. She barely touches his arm. They glide off with footfalls softened on the leaves, the old leaves powdered by a million satin slippers.

They are in a room. John knows nothing of it. Only, that the flesh and blood of Dorris are its walls. Singing walls. Lights, soft, as if they shine through clear pink fingers. Soft lights, and warm.

John reaches for a manuscript of his, and reads. Dorris, who has no eyes, has eyes to understand him. He comes to a dancing scene. The scene is Dorris. She dances. Dorris dances. Glorious Dorris. Dorris whirls, whirls, dances. . .

Dorris dances.
The pianist crashes a bumper chord. The whole stage claps. Dorris, flushed, looks quick at John. His whole face is in shadow. She seeks for her dance in it. She finds it a dead thing in the shadow which is his dream. She rushes from the stage. Falls down the steps into her dressing-room. Pulls her hair. Her eyes, over a floor of tears, stare at the whitewashed ceiling. (Smell of dry paste, and paint, and soiled clothing.) Her pal comes in. Dorris flings herself into the old safe arms, and cries bitterly.

"I told you nothin doin," is what Mame says to comfort her.

HER LIPS ARE COPPER WIRE

whisper of yellow globes
gleaming on lamp-posts that sway
like bootleg licker drinkers in the fog

and let your breath be moist against me
like bright beads on yellow globes

telephone the power-house
that the main wires are insulate

(her words play softly up and down
dewy corridors of billboards)

then with your tongue remove the tape
and press your lips to mine
till they are incandescent

CALLING JESUS

Her soul is like a little thrust-tailed dog that follows her, whimpering. She is large enough, I know, to find a warm spot for it. But each night when she comes home and closes the big outside storm door, the little dog is left in the vestibule, filled with chills till morning. Some one . . . eoho Jesus . . . soft as a cotton boll brushed against the milk-pod cheek of Christ, will steal in and cover it that it need not shiver, and carry it to her where she sleeps upon clean hay cut in her dreams.

When you meet her in the daytime on the streets, the little dog keeps coming. Nothing happens at first, and then, when she has forgotten the streets and alleys, and the large house where she goes to bed of nights, a soft thing like fur begins to rub your limbs, and you hear a low, scared voice, lonely, calling, and you know that a cool something nozzles moisture in your palms. Sensitive things like nostrils, quiver. Her breath comes sweet as honeysuckle whose pistils bear the life of coming song. And her eyes carry to where builders find no need for vestibules. For swinging on iron hinges, storm doors.

Her soul is like a little thrust-tailed dog, that follows her, whimpering. I've seen it tagging on behind her, up streets where chestnut trees flowered, where dusty asphalt had been freshly sprinkled with clean water. Up alleys where niggers sat on low door-steps before tumbled shanties and sang and loved. At night, when she comes home, the little dog is left in the vestibule, nosing the crack beneath the big storm door, filled with chills till morning. Some one . . . eoho Jesus . . . soft as the bare feet of Christ moving across bales of southern cotton, will steal in and cover it that it need not shiver, and carry it to her where she sleeps: cradled in dream-fluted cane.

BOX SEAT[1]

1

Houses are shy girls whose eyes shine reticently upon the dusk body of the street. Upon the gleaming limbs and asphalt torso of a dreaming nigger. Shake your curled wool-blossoms,[2] nigger. Open your liver lips[3] to the lean, white spring. Stir the root-life of a withered people. Call them from their houses, and teach them to dream.

Dark swaying forms of Negroes are street songs that woo virginal houses.

Dan Moore walks southward on Thirteenth Street.[4] The low limbs of budding chestnut trees recede above his head. Chestnut buds and blossoms are wool he walks upon. The eyes of houses faintly touch him as he passes them. Soft girl-eyes, they set him singing. Girl-eyes within him widen upward to promised faces. Floating away, they dally wistfully over the dusk body of the street. Come on, Dan Moore, come on. Dan sings. His voice is a little hoarse. It cracks. He strains to produce tones in keeping with the houses' loveliness. Cant be done. He whistles. His notes are shrill. They hurt him. Negroes open gates, and go indoors, perfectly. Dan thinks of the house he's going to. Of the girl. Lips, flesh-notes of a forgotten song, plead with him . . .

Dan turns into a side-street, opens an iron gate, bangs it to. Mounts the steps, and searches for the bell. Funny, he cant find it. He fumbles around. The thought comes to him that some one passing by might see him, and not understand. Might think that he is trying to sneak, to break in.

Dan: Break in. Get an ax and smash in. Smash in their faces. I'll show em. Break into an engine-house, steal a thousand horse-power fire truck. Smash in with the truck. I'll show em. Grab an ax and brain em. Cut em up. Jack the Ripper.[5] Baboon from the zoo. And then the cops come. "No, I aint a baboon. I aint Jack the Ripper. I'm a poor man out of work. Take your hands off me, you bull-necked bears. Look into my eyes. I am Dan Moore. I was born in a canefield. The hands of Jesus touched me. I am come to a sick world to heal it. Only the other day, a dope fiend brushed against me—Dont laugh, you mighty, juicy, meat-hook men. Give me your fingers and I will peel them as if they were ripe bananas."

Some one might think he is trying to break in. He'd better knock. His knuckles are raw bone against the thick glass door. He waits. No one comes. Perhaps they havent heard him. He raps again. This time, harder. He waits. No one comes. Some one is surely in. He fancies that he sees their shadows on the glass. Shadows of gorillas. Perhaps they saw him coming and dont want to let him in. He knocks. The tension of his arms makes the glass rattle. Hurried steps come towards him. The door opens.

"Please, you might break the glass—the bell—oh, Mr. Moore! I thought it must be some stranger. How do you do? Come in, wont you? Muriel? Yes. I'll call her. Take your things off, wont you? And have a seat in the parlor. Muriel will be right down. Muriel! Oh Muriel! Mr. Moore to see you. She'll be right down. You'll pardon me, wont you? So glad to see you."

Her eyes are weak. They are bluish and watery from reading newspapers. The blue is steel. It gimlets Dan while her
mouth flaps amiably to him.

Dan: Nothing for you to see, old musselhead. Dare I show
you? If I did, delirium would furnish you headlines for a
month. Now look here. Thats enough. Go long, woman. Say
some nasty thing and I'll kill you. Huh. Better damned sight
not. Ta-ta, Mrs. Pribby.

Mrs. Pribby retreats to the rear of the house. She takes up
a newspaper. There is a sharp click as she fits into her chair
and draws it to the table. The click is metallic like the sound
of a bolt being shot into place. Dan's eyes sting. Sinking
into a soft couch, he closes them. The house contracts about
him. It is a sharp-edged, massed, metallic house. Bolted.
About Mrs. Pribby. Bolted to the endless rows of metal
houses. Mrs. Pribby's house. The rows of houses belong to
other Mrs. Pribbys. No wonder he couldn't sing to them.

Dan: What's Muriel doing here? God, what a place for
her. Whats she doing? Putting her stockings on? In the bath-
room. Come out of there, Dan Moore. People must have
their privacy. Peeping-toms. I'll never peep. I'll listen. I like
to listen.

Dan goes to the wall and places his ear against it. A passing street car[6] and something vibrant from the earth sends a
rumble to him. That rumble comes from the earth's deep
core. It is the mutter of powerful underground races. Dan
has a picture of all the people rushing to put their ears
against walls, to listen to it. The next world-savior is coming
up that way. Coming up. A continent sinks down. The new-
world Christ will need consummate skill to walk upon the
waters where huge bubbles burst . . . Thuds of Muriel coming down. Dan turns to the piano and glances through a
stack of jazz music sheets. Ji-Ji-bo, JI-JI-BO!. .

"Hello, Dan, stranger, what brought you here?"

Muriel comes in, shakes hands, and then clicks into a high-armed seat under the orange glow of a floor-lamp. Her face is fleshy. It would tend to coarseness but for the fresh fragrant something which is the life of it. Her hair like an Indian's. But more curly and bushed and vagrant. Her nostrils flare. The flushed ginger of her cheeks is touched orange by the shower of color from the lamp.

"Well, you havent told me, you havent answered my question, stranger. What brought you here?"

Dan feels the pressure of the house, of the rear room, of the rows of houses, shift to Muriel. He is light. He loves her. He is doubly heavy.

"Dont know, Muriel—wanted to see you—wanted to talk to you—to see you and tell you that I know what you've been through—what pain the last few months must have been—"

"Lets dont mention that."

"But why not, Muriel? I—"

"Please."

"But Muriel, life is full of things like that. One grows strong and beautiful in facing them. What else is life?"

"I dont know, Dan. And I dont believe I care. Whats the use? Lets talk about something else. I hear there's a good show at the Lincoln[7] this week."

"Yes, so Harry was telling me. Going?"

"To-night."

Dan starts to rise.

"I didnt know. I dont want to keep you."

"Its all right. You dont have to go till Bernice comes. And she wont be here till eight. I'm all dressed. I'll let you know."

"Thanks."

Silence. The rustle of a newspaper being turned comes from the rear room.

Muriel: Shame about Dan. Something awfully good and fine about him. But he don't fit in. In where? Me? Dan, I could love you if I tried. I dont have to try. I do. O Dan, dont you know I do? Timid lover, brave talker that you are. Whats the good of all you know if you dont know that? I wont let myself. I? Mrs. Pribby who reads newspapers all night wont. What has she got to do with me? She *is* me, somehow. No she's not. Yes she is. She is the town, and the town wont let me love you, Dan. Dont you know? You could make it let me if you would. Why wont you? Youre selfish. I'm not strong enough to buck it. Youre too selfish to buck it, for me. I wish you'd go. You irritate me. Dan, please go.

"What are you doing now, Dan?"

"Same old thing, Muriel. Nothing, as the world would have it. Living, as I look at things. Living as much as I can without—"

"But you cant live without money, Dan. Why dont you get a good job and settle down?"

Dan: Same old line. Shoot it at me, sister. Hell of a note, this loving business. For ten minutes of it youve got to stand the torture of an intolerable heaviness and a hundred platitudes. Well, damit, shoot on.

"To what? my dear. Rustling newspapers?"

"You mustnt say that, Dan. It isnt right. Mrs. Pribby has been awfully good to me."

"Dare say she has. Whats that got to do with it?"

"Oh, Dan, youre so unconsiderate and selfish. All you think of is yourself."

"I think of you."

"Too much—I mean, you ought to work more and think less. Thats the best way to get along."

"Mussel-heads get along, Muriel. There is more to you than that—"

"Sometimes I think there is, Dan. But I dont know. I've tried. I've tried to do something with myself. Something real and beautiful, I mean. But whats the good of trying? I've tried to make people, every one I come in contact with, happy—"

Dan looks at her, directly. Her animalism, still unconquered by zoo-restrictions and keeper-taboos, stirs him. Passion tilts upward, bringing with it the elements of an old desire. Muriel's lips become the flesh-notes of a futile, plaintive longing. Dan's impulse to direct her is its fresh life.

"Happy, Muriel? No, not happy. Your aim is wrong. There is no such thing as happiness. Life bends joy and pain, beauty and ugliness, in such a way that no one may isolate them. No one should want to. Perfect joy, or perfect pain, with no contrasting element to define them, would mean a monotony of consciousness, would mean death. Not happy, Muriel. Say that you have tried to make them create. Say that you have used your own capacity for life to cradle them. To start them upward-flowing. Or if you cant say that you have, then say that you will. My talking to you will make you aware of your power to do so. Say that you will love, that you will give yourself in love—"

"To you, Dan?"

Dan's consciousness crudely swerves into his passions. They flare up in his eyes. They set up quivers in his abdomen. He is suddenly over-tense and nervous. .

"Muriel—"

The newspaper rustles in the rear room.

"Muriel—"

Dan rises. His arms stretch towards her. His fingers and his palms, pink in the lamplight, are glowing irons. Muriel's chair is close and stiff about her. The house, the rows of houses locked about her chair. Dan's fingers and arms are fire to melt and bars to wrench and force and pry. Her arms hang loose. Her hands are hot and moist. Dan takes them. He slips to his knees before her.

"Dan, you mustnt."

"Muriel—"

"Dan, really you mustnt. No, Dan. No."

"Oh, come, Muriel. Must I—"

"Shhh. Dan, please get up. Please. Mrs. Pribby is right in the next room. She'll hear you. She may come in. Dont, Dan. She'll see you—"

"Well then, lets go out."

"I cant. Let go, Dan. Oh, wont you please let go."

Muriel tries to pull her hands away. Dan tightens his grip. He feels the strength of his fingers. His muscles are tight and strong. He stands up. Thrusts out his chest. Muriel shrinks from him. Dan becomes aware of his crude absurdity. His lips curl. His passion chills. He has an obstinate desire to possess her.

"Muriel, I love you. I want you, whatever the world of Pribby says. Damn your Pribby. Who is she to dictate my love? I've stood enough of her. Enough of you. Come here."

Muriel's mouth works in and out. Her eyes flash and waggle. She wrenches her hands loose and forces them against his breast to keep him off. Dan grabs her wrists. Wedges in between her arms. Her face is close to him. It is hot and blue and moist. Ugly.

"Come here now."

"Dont, Dan. Oh, dont. What are you killing?"

"Whats weak in both of us and a whole litter of Pribbys. For once in your life youre going to face whats real, by God—"

A sharp rap on the newspaper in the rear room cuts between them. The rap is like cool thick glass between them.

Dan is hot on one side. Muriel, hot on the other. They straighten. Gaze fearfully at one another. Neither moves. A clock in the rear room, in the rear room, the rear room, strikes eight. Eight slow, cool sounds. Bernice. Muriel fastens on her image. She smooths her dress. She adjusts her skirt. She becomes prim and cool. Rising, she skirts Dan as if to keep the glass between them. Dan, gyrating nervously above the easy swing of his limbs, follows her to the parlor door. Muriel retreats before him till she reaches the landing of the steps that lead upstairs. She smiles at him. Dan sees his face in the hall mirror. He runs his fingers through his hair. Reaches for his hat and coat and puts them on. He moves towards Muriel. Muriel steps backward up one step. Dan's jaw shoots out. Muriel jerks her arm in warning of Mrs. Pribby. She gasps and turns and starts to run. Noise of a chair scraping as Mrs. Pribby rises from it, ratchets down the hall. Dan stops. He makes a wry face, wheels round, goes out, and slams the door.

2

People come in slowly . . . mutter, laughs, flutter, whishadwash,[8] "I've changed my work clothes—" . . . and fill vacant seats of Lincoln Theater. Muriel, leading Bernice who is a cross between a washerwoman and a blue-blood lady, a washer-blue, a washer-lady, wanders down the right aisle to the lower front box. Muriel has on an orange dress. Its color would clash with the crimson box-draperies,[9] its color would contradict the sweet rose smile her face is bathed in, should she take her coat off. She'll keep it on. Pale purple shadows rest on the planes of her cheeks. Deep purple comes from her thick-shocked hair. Orange of the dress goes well with these. Muriel presses her coat down from around her shoulders. Teachers are not supposed to have bobbed hair.[10] She'll keep her hat on. She takes the first chair, and indicates that Bernice is to take the one directly behind her. Seated thus, her eyes are level with, and near to, the face of an imaginary man upon the stage. To speak to Berny she must turn. When she does, the audience is square upon her.

People come in slowly . . . "—for my Sunday-go-to-meeting dress. O glory God! O shout Amen!" . . . and fill vacant seats of Lincoln Theater. Each one is a bolt that shoots into a slot, and is locked there. Suppose the Lord should ask, where was Moses when the light went out?[11] Suppose Gabriel should blow his trumpet![12] The seats are slots. The seats are bolted houses. The mass grows denser. Its weight at first is impalpable upon the box. Then Muriel begins to feel it. She props her arm against the brass box-rail, to ward it off. Silly. These people are friends of hers: a parent of a child she teaches, an old school friend. She smiles at them. They return her courtesy, and she is free to chat with Berny. Berny's tongue, started, runs on, and on. O washer-blue! O washer-lady!

Muriel: Never see Dan again. He makes me feel queer. Starts things he doesnt finish. Upsets me. I am not upset. I am perfectly calm. I am going to enjoy the show. Good show. I've had some show! This damn tame thing. O Dan. Wont see Dan again. Not alone. Have Mrs. Pribby come in. She *was* in. Keep Dan out. If I love him, can I keep him out? Well then, I dont love him. Now he's out. Who is that coming in? Blind as a bat. Ding-bat. Looks like Dan. He mustnt see me. Silly. He cant reach me. He wont dare come in here. He'd put his head down like a goring bull and charge me. He'd trample them. He'd gore. He'd rape! Berny! He won't dare come in here.

"Berny, who was that who just came in? I havent my glasses."

"A friend of yours, a *good* friend so I hear. Mr. Daniel Moore, Lord."

"Oh. He's no friend of mine."

"No? I hear he is."

"Well, he isnt."

Dan is ushered down the aisle. He has to squeeze past the knees of seated people to reach his own seat. He treads on a man's corns. The man grumbles, and shoves him off. He shrivels close beside a portly Negress whose huge rolls of flesh meet about the bones of seat-arms. A soil-soaked fragrance comes from her. Through the cement floor her strong roots sink down. They spread under the asphalt streets. Dreaming, the streets roll over on their bellies, and suck their glossy health from them. Her strong roots sink down and spread under the river and disappear in blood-lines that waver south. Her roots shoot down. Dan's hands follow them. Roots throb. Dan's heart beats violently. He places his palms upon the earth to cool them. Earth throbs. Dan's heart beats violently. He sees all the people in the house rush to the walls to listen to the rumble. A new-world Christ is coming up. Dan comes up. He is startled. The eyes of the woman dont belong to her. They look at him unpleasantly. From either aisle, bolted masses press in. He doesnt fit. The mass grows agitant. For an instant, Dan's and Muriel's eyes meet. His weight there slides the weight on her. She braces an arm against the brass rail, and turns her head away.

Muriel: Damn fool; dear Dan, what did you want to follow me here for? Oh cant you ever do anything right? Must you always pain me, and make me hate you? I do hate you. I wish some one would come in with a horse-whip and lash you out. I wish some one would drag you up a back alley and brain you with the whip-butt.

Muriel glances at her wrist-watch.

"Quarter of nine. Berny, what time have you?"

"Eight-forty. Time to begin. Oh, look Muriel, that woman with the plume; doesnt she look good! They say she's going with, oh, whats his name. You know. Too much powder.[13] I can see it from here. Here's the orchestra now. O fine! Jim Clem at the piano!"

The men fill the pit. Instruments run the scale and tune. The saxophone moans and throws a fit. Jim Clem, poised over the piano, is ready to begin. His head nods forward. Opening crash. The house snaps dark. The curtain recedes upward from the blush of the footlights. Jazz overture is over. The first act is on.

Dan: Old stuff. Muriel—bored. Must be. But she'll smile and she'll clap. Do what youre bid, you she-slave. Look at her. Sweet, tame woman in a brass box seat. Clap, smile, fawn, clap. Do what youre bid. Drag me in with you. Dirty me. Prop me in your brass box seat. I'm there, am I not? because of you. He-slave. Slave of a woman who is a slave. I'm a damned sight worse than you are. I sing your praises, Beauty! I exalt thee, O Muriel! A slave, thou art greater than all Freedom because I love thee.

Dan fidgets, and disturbs his neighbors. His neighbors glare at him. He glares back without seeing them. The man whose corns have been trod upon speaks to him.

"Keep quiet, cant you, mister. Other people have paid their money besides yourself to see the show."

The man's face is a blur about two sullen liquid things that are his eyes. The eyes dissolve in the surrounding vagueness. Dan suddenly feels that the man is an enemy whom he has long been looking for.

Dan bristles. Glares furiously at the man.

"All right. All right then. Look at the show. I'm not stopping you."

"Shhh," from some one in the rear.

Dan turns around.

"Its that man there who started everything I didnt say a thing to him until he tried to start something. What have I got to do with whether he has paid his money or not? Thats the manager's business. Do I look like the manager?"

"Shhhh. Youre right. Shhhh."

"Dont tell me to shhh. Tell him. That man there. He started everything. If what he wanted was to start a fight, why didnt he say so?"

The man leans forward.

"Better be quiet, sonny. I aint said a thing about fight, yet."

"Its a good thing you havent."

"Shhhh."

Dan grips himself. Another act is on. Dwarfs, dressed like prize-fighters, foreheads bulging like boxing gloves, are led upon the stage. They are going to fight for the heavyweight championship. Gruesome. Dan glances at Muriel. He imagines that she shudders. His mind curves back into himself, and picks up tail-ends of experiences. His eyes are open, mechanically. The dwarfs pound and bruise and bleed each other, on his eyeballs.

Dan: Ah, but she was some baby! And not vulgar either. Funny how some women can do those things. Muriel dancing like that! Hell. She rolled and wabbled. Her buttocks rocked. She pulled up her dress and showed her pink drawers. Baby! And then she caught my eyes. Dont know what my eyes had in them. Yes I do. God, dont I though! Sometimes I think, Dan Moore, that your eyes could burn clean . . . burn clean . . . BURN CLEAN! . .

The gong rings. The dwarfs set to. They spar grotesquely, playfully, until one lands a stiff blow. This makes the other sore. He commences slugging. A real scrap is on. Time! The dwarfs go to their corners and are sponged and fanned off. Gloves bulge from their wrists. Their wrists are necks for the tightfaced gloves. The fellow to the right lets his eyes roam over the audience. He sights Muriel. He grins.

Dan: Those silly women arguing feminism. Here's what I should have said to them. "It should be clear to you women, that the proposition must be stated thus:

> Me, horizontally above her.
> Action: perfect strokes downward oblique.
> Hence, man dominates because of limitation.
> Or, so it shall be until women learn their stuff.

So framed, the proposition is a mental-filler, Dentist, I want gold teeth. It should become cherished of the technical intellect. I hereby offer it to posterity as one of the important machine-age designs. P. S. It should be noted, that because it *is* an achievement of this age, its growth and hence its causes, up to the point of maturity, antedate machinery. Ery . . ."[14]

The gong rings. No fooling this time. The dwarfs set to. They clinch. The referee parts them. One swings a cruel upper-cut and knocks the other down. A huge head hits the floor. Pop! The house roars. The fighter, groggy, scrambles up. The referee whispers to the contenders not to fight so hard. They ignore him. They charge. Their heads jab like boxing-gloves. They kick and spit and bite. They pound each other furiously. Muriel pounds. The house pounds. Cut lips. Bloody noses. The referee asks for the gong. Time! The house roars. The dwarfs bow, are made to bow. The house wants more. The dwarfs are led from the stage.

Dan: Strange I never really noticed him before. Been sitting there for years. Born a slave. Slavery not so long ago. He'll die in his chair. Swing low, sweet chariot. Jesus will come and roll him down the river Jordan. Oh, come along, Moses, you'll get lost; stretch out your rod and come across. LET MY PEOPLE GO![15] Old man. Knows everyone who passes the corners. Saw the first horse-cars.[16] The first Oldsmobile. And he was born in slavery. I did see his eyes. Never miss eyes. But they were bloodshot and watery. It hurt to look at them. It hurts to look in most people's eyes. He saw Grant and Lincoln. He saw Walt—old man, did you see Walt Whitman?[17] Did you see Walt Whitman! Strange force that drew me to him. And I went up to see. The woman thought I saw crazy. I told him to look into the heavens. He did, and smiled. I asked him if he knew what that rumbling is that comes up from the ground. Christ, what a stroke that was. And the jabbering idiots crowding around. And the crossing-cop leaving his job to come over and wheel him away . . .

The house applauds. The house wants more. The dwarfs are led back. But no encore. Must give the house something. The attendant comes out and announces that Mr. Barry, the champion, will sing one of his own songs, "for your approval." Mr. Barry grins at Muriel as he wabbles from the wing. He holds a fresh white rose, and a small mirror. He wipes blood from his nose. He signals Jim Clem. The orchestra starts. A sentimental love song, Mr. Barry sings, first to one girl, and then another in the audience. He holds the mirror in such a way that it flashes in the face of each one he sings to. The light swings around.

Dan: I am going to reach up and grab the girders of this building and pull them down. The crash will be a signal. Hid by the smoke and dust Dan Moore will arise. In his right hand will be a dynamo.[18] In his left, a god's face that will flash white light from ebony. I'll grab a girder and swing it like a walking-stick. Lightning will flash. I'll grab its black knob and swing it like a crippled cane. Lightning . . . Some one's flashing . . . some one's flashing . . . Who in hell is flashing that mirror? Take it off me, godam you.

Dan's eyes are half blinded. He moves his head. The light follows. He hears the audience laugh. He hears the orchestra. A man with a high-pitched, sentimental voice is singing. Dan sees the dwarf. Along the mirror flash the song comes. Dan ducks his head. The audience roars. The light swings around to Muriel. Dan looks. Muriel is too close. Mr. Barry covers his mirror. He sings to her. She shrinks away. Nausea. She clutches the brass box-rail. She moves to face away. The audience is square upon her. Its eyes smile. Its hands itch to clap. Muriel turns to the dwarf and forces a smile at him. With a showy blare of orchestration, the song comes to its close. Mr. Barry bows. He offers Muriel the rose, first having kissed it. Blood of his battered lips is a vivid stain upon its petals. Mr. Barry offers Muriel the rose. The house applauds. Muriel flinches back. The dwarf steps forward, diffident; threatening. Hate pops from his eyes and crackles like a brittle heat about the box. The thick hide of his face is drawn in tortured wrinkles. Above his eyes, the bulging, tightskinned brow. Dan looks at it. It grows calm and massive. It grows profound. It is a thing of wisdom and tenderness, of suffering and beauty. Dan looks down. The eyes are calm and luminous. Words come from them . . . Arms of the audience reach out, grab Muriel, and hold her there. Claps are steel fingers that manacle her wrists and move them forward to acceptance. Berny leans forward and whispers:

"Its all right. Go on—take it."

Words form in the eyes of the dwarf:

> Do not shrink. Do not be afraid of me.
> *Jesus*
> See how my eyes look at you.

the Son of God
I too was made in His image.
was once—
I give you the rose.

Muriel, tight in her revulsion, sees black, and daintily reaches for the offering. As her hand touches it, Dan springs up in his seat and shouts:

"JESUS WAS ONCE A LEPER!"

Dan steps down.

He is as cool as a green stem that has just shed its flower.

Rows of gaping faces strain towards him. They are distant, beneath him, impalpable. Squeezing out, Dan again treads upon the cornfoot man. The man shoves him.

"Watch where youre going, mister. Crazy or no, you aint going to walk over me. Watch where youre going there."

Dan turns, and serenely tweaks the fellow's nose. The man jumps up. Dan is jammed against a seat-back. A slight swift anger flicks him. His fist hooks the other's jaw.

"Now you have started something. Aint no man living can hit me and get away with it. Come on on the outside."

The house, tumultuously stirring, grabs its wraps and follows the men.

The man leads Dan up a black alley. The alley-air is thick and moist with smells of garbage and wet trash. In the morning, singing niggers will drive by and ring their gongs . . . Heavy with the scent of rancid flowers and with the scent of fight. The crowd, pressing forward, is a hollow roar. Eyes of houses, soft girl-eyes, glow reticently upon the hubbub and blink out. The man stops. Takes off his hat and coat. Dan, having forgotten him, keeps going on.

PRAYER

My body is opaque to the soul.
Driven of the spirit, long have I sought to temper it unto the
    spirit's longing,
But my mind, too, is opaque to the soul.
A closed lid is my soul's flesh-eye.
O Spirits of whom my soul is but a little finger.
Direct it to the lid of its flesh-eye.
I am weak with much giving.
I am weak with the desire to give more.
(How strong a thing is the little finger!)
So weak that I have confused the body with the soul,
And the body with its little finger.
(How frail is the little finger.)
My voice could not carry to you did you dwell in stars,
O Spirits of whom my soul is but a little finger . .

HARVEST SONG

I am a reaper whose muscles set at sundown. All my oats are
   cradled.
But I am too chilled, and too fatigued to bind them. And I
   hunger.

I crack a grain between my teeth. I do not taste it.
I have been in the fields all day. My throat is dry. I hunger.

My eyes are caked with dust of oatfields at harvest-time.
I am a blind man who stares across the hills, seeking stack'd
   fields of other harvesters.

It would be good to see them . . crook'd, split, and iron-ring'd
   handles of the scythes. It would be good to see them, dust-
   caked and blind. I hunger.

(Dusk is a strange fear'd sheath their blades are dull'd in.)
My throat is dry. And should I call, a cracked grain like the
   oats . . . eoho—

I fear to call. What should they hear me, and offer me their
   grain, oats, or wheat, or corn? I have been in the fields all
   day. I fear I could not taste it. I fear knowledge of my hunger.

My ears are caked with dust of oatfields at harvest-time.
I am a deaf man who strains to hear the calls of other
    harvesters whose throats are also dry.

It would be good to hear their songs . . reapers of the sweet-
    stalk'd cane, cutters of the corn . . even though their throats
    cracked and the strangeness of their voices deafened me.

I hunger. My throat is dry. Now that the sun has set and I am
    chilled, I fear to call. (Eoho, my brothers!)

I am a reaper. (Eoho!) All my oats are cradled. But I am too
    fatigued to bind them. And I hunger. I crack a grain. It has
    no taste to it. My throat is dry . . .

O my brothers, I beat my palms, still soft, against the stubble
    of my harvesting. (You beat your soft palms, too.) My pain
    is sweet. Sweeter than the oats or wheat or corn. It will not
    bring me knowledge of my hunger.

BONA AND PAUL

1

On the school gymnasium floor, young men and women are drilling. They are going to be teachers, and go out into the world . . thud, thud . . and give precision to the movements of sick people who all their lives have been drilling. One man is out of step. In step. The teacher glares at him. A girl in bloomers,[1] seated on a mat in the corner because she has told the director that she is sick, sees that the footfalls of the men[2] are rhythmical and syncopated. The dance of his blue-trousered limbs thrills her.

Bona: He is a candle that dances in a grove swung with pale balloons.

Columns of the drillers thud towards her. He is in the front row. He is in no row at all. Bona can look close at him. His red-brown face—

Bona: He is a harvest moon. He is an autumn leaf. He is a nigger. Bona! But dont all the dorm girls say so? And dont you, when you are sane, say so? Thats why I love—Oh, nonsense. You have never loved a man who didnt first love you. Besides—

Columns thud away from her. Come to a halt in line formation. Rigid. The period bell rings, and the teacher dismisses them.

A group collects around Paul. They are choosing sides for basket-ball. Girls against boys. Paul has his. He is limbering up beneath the basket. Bona runs to the girl captain and asks to be chosen. The girls fuss. The director comes to quiet them. He hears what Bona wants.

"But, Miss Hale, you were excused—"

"So I was, Mr. Boynton, but—"

"—you can play basket-ball, but you are too sick to drill."

"If you wish to put it that way."

She swings away from him to the girl captain.

"Helen, I want to play, and you must let me. This is the first time I've asked and I dont see why—"

"Thats just it, Bona. We have our team."

"Well, team or no team, I want to play and thats all there is to it."

She snatches the ball from Helen's hands, and charges down the floor.

Helen shrugs. One of the weaker girls says that she'll drop out. Helen accepts this. The team is formed. The whistle blows. The game starts. Bona, in center, is jumping against Paul. He plays with her. Out-jumps her, makes a quick pass, gets a quick return, and shoots a goal from the middle of the floor. Bona burns crimson. She fights, and tries to guard him. One of her team-mates advises her not to play so hard. Paul shoots his second goal.

Bona begins to feel a little dizzy and all in. She drives on. Almost hugs Paul to guard him. Near the basket, he attempts to shoot, and Bona lunges into his body and tries to beat his arms. His elbow, going up, gives her a sharp crack on the jaw. She whirls. He catches her. Her body stiffens. Then becomes strangely vibrant, and bursts to a swift life within her anger. He is about to give way before her hatred when a new passion flares at him and makes his stomach fall. Bona squeezes him. He suddenly feels stifled, and wonders why in hell the ring of silly gaping faces that's caked about him doesnt make way and give him air. He has a swift illusion that it is himself who has been struck. He looks at Bona. Whir. Whir. They seem to be human distortions spinning tensely in a fog. Spinning . . dizzy . . spinning . . . Bona jerks herself free, flushes a startling crimson, breaks through the bewildered teams, and rushes from the hall.

2

Paul is in his room of two windows.

Outside, the South-Side L track³ cuts them in two.

Bona is one window. One window, Paul.

Hurtling Loop-jammed L trains⁴ throw them in swift shadow.

Paul goes to his. Gray slanting roofs of houses are tinted lavender in the setting sun. Paul follows the sun, over the stock-yards⁵ where a fresh stench is just arising, across wheat lands that are still waving above their stubble, into the sun. Paul follows the sun to a pine-matted hillock in Georgia. He sees the slanting roofs of gray unpainted cabins tinted lavender. A Negress chants a lullaby beneath the mate-eyes of a southern planter. Her breasts are ample for the suckling of a song. She weans it, and sends it, curiously weaving, among lush melodies of cane and corn. Paul follows the sun into himself in Chicago.

He is at Bona's window.

With his own glow he looks through a dark pane.

Paul's room-mate comes in.

"Say, Paul, I've got a date for you. Come on. Shake a leg, will you?"

His blonde hair is combed slick. His vest is snug about him. He is like the electric light which he snaps on.

"Whatdoysay, Paul? Get a wiggle on. Come on. We havent got much time by the time we eat and dress and everything."

His bustling concentrates on the brushing of his hair.

Art: What in hell's getting into Paul of late, anyway? Christ, but he's getting moony. Its his blood. Dark blood: moony. Doesnt get anywhere unless you boost it. You've got to keep it going—

"Say, Paul!"

—or it'll go to sleep on you. Dark blood; nigger? Thats what those jealous she-hens say. Not Bona though, or she . . from the South . . wouldnt want me to fix a date for him and her. Hell of a thing, that Paul's dark: you've got to always be answering questions.

"Say, Paul, for Christ's sake leave that window, cant you?"

"Whats it, Art?"

"Hell, I've told you about fifty times. Got a date for you. Come on."

"With who?"

Art: He didnt use to ask; now he does. Getting up in the air. Getting funny.

"Heres your hat. Want a smoke? Paul! Here. I've got a match. Now come on and I'll tell you all about it on the way to supper."

Paul: He's going to Life this time. No doubt of that. Quit your kidding. Some day, dear Art, I'm going to kick the living slats out of you, and you wont know what I've done it for. And your slats will bring forth Life . . beautiful woman . . .

Pure Food Restaurant.

"Bring me some soup with a lot of crackers, understand? And then a roast-beef dinner. Same for you, eh, Paul? Now as I was saying, you've got a swell chance with her. And she's game. Best proof: she dont give a damn what the dorm girls say about you and her in the gym, or about the funny looks that Boynton gives her, or about what they say about, well, hell, you know, Paul. And say, Paul, she's a sweetheart. Tall, not puffy and pretty, more serious and deep—the kind you like these days. And they say she's got a car. And say, she's on fire. But you know all about that. She got Helen to fix it up with me. The four of us—remember the last party? Crimson Gardens! Boy!"

Paul's eyes take on a light that Art can settle in.

3

Art has on his patent-leather pumps and fancy vest. A loose fall coat is swung across his arm. His face has been massaged, and over a close shave, powdered. It is a healthy pink the blue of evening tints a purple pallor. Art is happy and confident in the good looks that his mirror gave him. Bubbling over with a joy he must spend now if the night is to contain it all. His bubbles, too, are curiously tinted purple as Paul watches them. Paul, contrary to what he had thought he would be like, is cool like the dusk, and like the dusk, detached. His dark face is a floating shade in evening's shadow. He sees Art, curiously. Art is a purple fluid, carbon-charged, that effervesces beside him. He loves Art. But is it not queer, this pale purple facsimile of a red-blooded Norwegian friend of his? Perhaps for some reason, white skins are not supposed to live at night. Surely, enough nights would transform them fantastically, or kill them. And their red passion? Night paled that too, and made it moony. Moony. Thats what Art thought of him. Bona didnt, even in the daytime. Bona, would she be pale? Impossible. Not that red glow. But the conviction did not set his emotion flowing.

"Come right in, wont you? The young ladies will be right down. Oh, Mr. Carlstrom, do play something for us while you are waiting. We just love to listen to your music. You play so well."

Houses, and dorm sitting-rooms are places where white faces seclude themselves at night. There is a reason . . .

Art sat on the piano and simply tore it down. Jazz. The picture of Our Poets[6] hung perilously.

Paul: I've got to get the kid to play that stuff for me in the daytime. Might be different. More himself. More nigger. Different? There is. Curious, though.

The girls come in. Art stops playing, and almost immediately takes up a petty quarrel, where he had last left it, with Helen.

Bona, black-hair curled staccato, sharply contrasting with Helen's puffy yellow, holds Paul's hand. She squeezes it. Her own emotion supplements the return pressure. And then, for no tangible reason, her spirits drop. Without them, she is nervous, and slightly afraid. She resents this. Paul's eyes are critical. She resents Paul. She flares at him. She flares to poise and security.

"Shall we be on our way?"

"Yes, Bona, certainly."

The Boulevard is sleek in asphalt, and, with arc-lights and limousines, aglow. Dry leaves scamper behind the whir of cars. The scent of exploded gasoline that mingles with them is faintly sweet. Mellow stone mansions overshadow clapboard homes which now resemble Negro shanties in some southern alley. Bona and Paul, and Art and Helen, move along an island-like, far-stretching strip of leaf-soft ground.

Above them, worlds of shadow-planes and solids, silently moving. As if on one of these, Paul looks down on Bona. No doubt of it: her face is pale. She is talking. Her words have no feel to them. One sees them. They are pink petals that fall upon velvet cloth. Bona is soft, and pale, and beautiful.

"Paul, tell me something about yourself—or would you rather wait?"

"I'll tell you anything you'd like to know."

"Not what I want to know, Paul; what you want to tell me."

"You have the beauty of a gem fathoms under sea."

"I feel that, but I dont want to be. I want to be near you. Perhaps I will be if I tell you something. Paul, I love you."

The sea casts up its jewel into his hands, and burns them furiously. To tuck her arm under his and hold her hand will ease the burn.

"What can I say to you, brave dear woman—I cant talk love. Love is a dry grain in my mouth unless it is wet with kisses."

"You would dare? right here on the Boulevard? before Arthur and Helen?"

"Before myself? I dare."

"Here then."

Bona, in the slim shadow of a tree trunk, pulls Paul to her. Suddenly she stiffens. Stops.

"But you have not said you love me."

"I cant—yet—Bona."

"Ach, you never will. Youre cold. Cold."

Bona: Colored; cold. Wrong somewhere.

She hurries and catches up with Art and Helen.

4

Crimson Gardens. Hurrah! So one feels. People . . . University of Chicago students, members of the stock exchange, a large Negro in crimson uniform who guards the door[7] . . had watched them enter. Had leaned towards each other over ash-smeared tablecloths and highballs and whispered: What is he, a Spaniard, an Indian, an Italian, a Mexican, a Hindu, or a Japanese? Art had at first fidgeted under their stares . . what are *you* looking at, you godam pack of owl-eyed hyenas? . . but soon settled into his fuss with Helen, and forgot them. A strange thing happened to Paul. Suddenly he knew that he was apart from the people around him. Apart from the pain which they had unconsciously caused. Suddenly he knew that people saw, not attractiveness in his dark skin, but difference. Their stares, giving him to himself, filled something long empty within him, and were like green blades sprouting in his consciousness. There was fullness, and strength and peace about it all. He saw himself, cloudy, but real. He saw the faces of the people at the tables round him. White lights, or as now, the pink lights of the Crimson Gardens gave a glow and immediacy to white faces. The pleasure of it, equal to that of love or dream, of seeing this. Art and Bona and Helen? He'd look. They were wonderfully flushed and beautiful. Not for himself; because they were. Distantly. Who were they, anyway? God, if he knew them. He'd come in with them. Of that he was sure. Come where? Into life? Yes. No. Into the Crimson Gardens. A part of life. A carbon bubble. Would it look purple if he went out into the night and looked at it? His sudden starting to rise almost upset the table.

"What in hell—pardon—whats the matter, Paul?"

"I forgot my cigarettes—"

"Youre smoking one."

"So I am. Pardon me.'

The waiter straightens them out. Takes their order.

Art: What in hell's eating Paul? Moony aint the word for it. From bad to worse. And those godam people staring so. Paul's a queer fish. Doesnt seem to mind . . . He's my pal, let me tell you, you horn-rimmed owl-eyed hyena at that table, and a lot better than you whoever you are . . . Queer about him. I could stick up for him if he'd only come out, one way or the other, and tell a feller. Besides, a room-mate has a right to know. Thinks I wont understand. Said so. He's got a swell head when it comes to brains, all right. God, he's a good straight feller, though. Only, moony. Nut. Nuttish. Nuttery. Nutmeg . . . "What'd you say, Helen?"

"I was talking to Bona, thank you."

"Well, its nothing to get spiffy about."

"What? Oh, of course not. Please lets dont start some silly argument all over again."

"Well."

"Well."

"Now thats enough. Say, waiter, whats the matter with our order? Make it snappy, will you?"

Crimson Gardens. Hurrah! So one feels. The drinks come. Four highballs. Art passes cigarettes. A girl dressed like a bare-back rider in flaming pink, makes her way through tables to the dance floor. All lights are dimmed till they seem a lush afterglow of crimson. Spotlights the girl. She sings. "Liza, Little Liza Jane."[8]

Paul is rosy before his window.

He moves, slightly, towards Bona.

With his own glow, he seeks to penetrate a dark pane.

Paul: From the South. What does that mean, precisely, except that you'll love or hate a nigger? Thats a lot. What does it mean except that in Chicago you'll have the courage to neither love or hate. A priori. But it would seem that you have. Queer words, arent these, for a man who wears blue pants on a gym floor in the daytime. Well, never matter. You matter. I'd like to know you whom I look at. Know, not love. Not that knowing is a greater pleasure; but that I have just found the joy of it. You came just a month too late. Even this afternoon I dreamed. To-night, along the Boulevard, you found me cold. Paul Johnson, cold! Thats a good one, eh, Art, you fine old stupid fellow, you! But I feel good! The color and the music and the song . . . A Negress chants a lullaby beneath the mate-eyes of a southern planter. O song! . . And those flushed faces. Eager brilliant eyes. Hard to imagine them as unawakened. Your own. Oh, they're awake all right. "And you know it too, dont you Bona?"

"What, Paul?"

"The truth of what I was thinking."

"I'd like to know I know—something of you."

"You will—before the evening's over. I promise it."

Crimson Gardens. Hurrah! So one feels. The bare-back rider balances agilely on the applause which is the tail of her song. Orchestral instruments warm up for jazz. The flute is a cat that ripples its fur against the deep-purring saxophone. The drum throws sticks. The cat jumps on the piano keyboard. Hi diddle, hi diddle, the cat and the fiddle. Crimson Gardens . . hurrah! . . jumps over the moon. Crimson Gardens! Helen . . O Eliza . . rabbit-eyes sparkling, plays up to, and tries to placate what she considers to be Paul's contempt. She always does that . . Little Liza Jane . . . Once home, she burns with the thought of what she's done. She says all manner of snidy things about him, and swears that she'll never go out again when he is along. She tries to get Art to break with him, saying, that if Paul, whom the whole dormitory calls a nigger, is more to him than she is, well, she's through. She does not break with Art. She goes out as often as she can with Art and Paul. She explains this to herself by a piece of information which a friend of hers had given her: men like him (Paul) can fascinate. One is not responsible for fascination. Not one girl had really loved Paul; he fascinated them. Bona didnt; only thought she did. Time would tell. And of course, *she* didnt. Liza . . . She plays up to, and tries to placate, Paul.

"Paul is so deep these days, and I'm so glad he's found some one to interest him."

"I dont believe I do."

The thought escapes from Bona just a moment before her anger at having said it.

Bona: You little puffy cat, I do. I do!

Dont I, Paul? her eyes ask.

Her answer is a crash of jazz from the palm-hidden orchestra. Crimson Gardens is a body whose blood flows to a clot upon the dance floor. Art and Helen clot. Soon, Bona and Paul. Paul finds her a little stiff, and his mind, wandering to Helen (silly little kid who wants every highball spoon her hands touch, for a souvenir), supple, perfect little dancer, wishes for the next dance when he and Art will exchange.

Bona knows that she must win him to herself.

"Since when have men like you grown cold?"

"The first philosopher."

"I thought you were a poet—or a gym director."

"Hence, your failure to make love."

Bona's eyes flare. Water. Grow red about the rims. She would like to tear away from him and dash across the clotted floor.

"What do you mean?"

"Mental concepts rule you. If they were flush with mine—good. I dont believe they are."

"How do you know, Mr. Philosopher?"

"Mostly a priori."[9]

"You talk well for a gym director."

"And you—"

"I hate you. Ou!"

She presses away. Paul, conscious of the convention in it, pulls her to him. Her body close. Her head still strains away. He nearly crushes her. She tries to pinch him. Then sees people staring, and lets her arms fall. Their eyes meet. Both, contemptuous. The dance takes blood from their minds and packs it, tingling, in the torsos of their swaying bodies. Passionate blood leaps back into their eyes. They are a dizzy blood clot on a gyrating floor. They know that the pink-faced people have no part in what they feel. Their instinct leads them away from Art and Helen, and towards the big uniformed black man who opens and closes the gilded exit door. The cloak-room girl is tolerant of their impatience over such trivial things as wraps. And slightly superior. As the black man swings the door for them, his eyes are knowing. Too many couples have passed out, flushed and fidgety, for him not to know. The chill air is a shock to Paul. A strange thing happens. He sees the Gardens purple, as if he were way off. And a spot is in the purple. The spot comes furiously towards him. Face of the black man. It leers. It smiles sweetly like a child's. Paul leaves Bona and darts back so quickly that he doesnt give the door-man a chance to open. He swings in. Stops. Before the huge bulk of the Negro.

"Youre wrong."

"Yassur."

"Brother, youre wrong.

"I came back to tell you, to shake your hand, and tell you that you are wrong. That something beautiful is going to happen. That the Gardens are purple like a bed of roses would be at dusk. That I came into the Gardens, into life in the Gardens with one whom I did not know. That I danced with her, and did not know her. That I felt passion, contempt and passion for her whom I did not know. That I thought of her. That my thoughts were matches thrown into a dark window. And all the while the Gardens were purple like a bed of roses would be at dusk. I came back to tell you, brother, that white faces are petals of roses. That dark faces are petals of dusk. That I am going out and gather petals. That I am going out and know her whom I brought here with me to these Gardens which are purple like a bed of roses would be at dusk."

Paul and the black man shook hands.

When he reached the spot where they had been standing, Bona was gone.

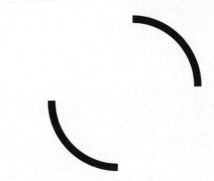

To Waldo Frank.[1]

KABNIS

1

Ralph Kabnis, propped in his bed, tries to read. To read himself to sleep. An oil lamp on a chair near his elbow burns unsteadily. The cabin room is spaced fantastically about it. Whitewashed hearth and chimney, black with sooty saw-teeth. Ceiling, patterned by the fringed globe of the lamp. The walls, unpainted, are seasoned a rosin yellow. And cracks between the boards are black. These cracks are the lips the night winds use for whispering. Night winds in Georgia are vagrant poets, whispering. Kabnis, against his will, lets his book slip down, and listens to them. The warm whiteness of his bed, the lamp-light, do not protect him from the weird chill of their song:

> White-man's land.
> Niggers, sing.
> Burn, bear black children
> Till poor rivers bring
> Rest, and sweet glory
> In Camp Ground.[2]

Kabnis' thin hair is streaked on the pillow. His hand strokes the slim silk of his mustache. His thumb, pressed under his chin, seems to be trying to give squareness and projection to it. Brown eyes stare from a lemon face. Moisture gathers beneath his arm-pits. He slides down beneath the cover, seeking release.

Kabnis: Near me. Now. Whoever you are, my warm glowing sweetheart, do not think that the face that rests beside you is the real Kabnis. Ralph Kabnis is a dream. And dreams are faces with large eyes and weak chins and broad brows that get smashed by the fists of square faces. The body of the world is bull-necked. A dream is a soft face that fits uncertainly upon it . . . God, if I could develop that in words. Give what I know a bull-neck and a heaving body, all would go well with me, wouldnt it, sweetheart? If I could feel that I came to the South to face it. If I, the dream (not what is weak and afraid in me) could become the face of the South. How my lips would sing for it, my songs being the lips of its soul. Soul. Soul hell. There aint no such thing. What in hell was that?

A rat had run across the thin boards of the ceiling. Kabnis thrusts his head out from the covers. Through the cracks, a powdery faded red dust sprays down on him. Dust of slave-fields, dried, scattered . . . No use to read. Christ, if he only could drink himself to sleep. Something as sure as fate was going to happen. He couldnt stand this thing much longer. A hen, perched on a shelf in the adjoining room begins to tread. Her nails scrape the soft wood. Her feathers ruffle.

"Get out of that, you egg-laying bitch."

Kabnis hurls a slipper against the wall. The hen flies from her perch and cackles as if a skunk were after her.

"Now cut out that racket or I'll wring your neck for you."

Answering cackles arise in the chicken yard.

"Why in Christ's hell cant you leave me alone? Damn it, I wish your cackle would choke you. Choke every mother's son

of them in this God-forsaken hole. Go away. By God I'll wring
your neck for you if you dont. Hell of a mess I've got in: even
the poultry is hostile. Go way. Go way. By God, I'll . . ."

Kabnis jumps from his bed. His eyes are wild. He makes
for the door. Bursts through it. The hen, driving blindly at
the windowpane, screams. Then flies and flops around trying to elude him. Kabnis catches her.

"Got you now, you she-bitch."

With his fingers about her neck, he thrusts open the outside door and steps out into the serene loveliness of Georgian
autumn moonlight. Some distance off, down in the valley, a
band of pine-smoke, silvered gauze, drifts steadily. The half-
moon is a white child that sleeps upon the tree-tops of the
forest. White winds croon its sleep-song:

> rock a-by baby . .[3]
> Black mother sways, holding a white child on her bosom.
> when the bough bends . .
> Her breath hums through pine-cones.
> cradle will fall . .
> Teat moon-children at your breasts,
> down will come baby . .
> Black mother.

Kabnis whirls the chicken by its neck, and throws the head
away. Picks up the hopping body, warm, sticky, and hides it
in a clump of bushes. He wipes blood from his hands onto
the coarse scant grass.

Kabnis: Thats done. Old Chromo[4] in the big house there
will wonder whats become of her pet hen. Well, it'll teach
her a lesson: not to make a hen-coop of my quarters. Quarters. Hell of a fine quarters, I've got. Five years ago; look at
me now. Earth's child. The earth my mother. God is a

profligate red-nosed man about town. Bastardy; me. A bastard son has got a right to curse his maker. God . . .

Kabnis is about to shake his fists heavenward. He looks up, and the night's beauty strikes him dumb. He falls to his knees. Sharp stones cut through his thin pajamas. The shock sends a shiver over him. He quivers. Tears mist his eyes. He writhes.

"God Almighty, dear God, dear Jesus, do not torture me with beauty. Take it away. Give me an ugly world. Ha, ugly. Stinking like unwashed niggers. Dear Jesus, do not chain me to myself and set these hills and valleys, heaving with folksongs, so close to me that I cannot reach them. There is a radiant beauty in the night that touches and . . . tortures me. Ugh. Hell. Get up, you damn fool. Look around. Whats beautiful there? Hog pens and chicken yards. Dirty red mud. Stinking outhouse. Whats beauty anyway but ugliness if it hurts you? God, he doesnt exist, but nevertheless He is ugly. Hence, what comes from Him is ugly. Lynchers and business men, and that cockroach Hanby, especially. How come that he gets to be principal of a school? Of the school I'm driven to teach in? God's handiwork, doubtless. God and Hanby, they belong together. Two godam moral-spouters. Oh, no, I wont let that emotion come up in me. Stay down. Stay down, I tell you. O Jesus, Thou art beautiful . . . Come, Ralph, pull yourself together. Curses and adoration dont come from what is sane. This loneliness, dumbness, awful, intangible oppression is enough to drive a man insane. Miles from nowhere. A speck on a Georgia hillside. Jesus, can you imagine it—an atom of dust in agony on a hillside? Thats a spectacle for you. Come, Ralph, old man, pull yourself together."

Kabnis has stiffened. He is conscious now of the night wind, and of how it chills him. He rises. He totters as a man would who for the first time uses artificial limbs. As a completely artificial man would. The large frame house, squatting on brick pillars, where the principal of the school, his wife, and the boarding girls sleep, seems a curious shadow of his mind. He tries, but cannot convince himself of its reality. His gaze drifts down into the vale, across the swamp, up over the solid dusk bank of pines, and rests, bewildered-like, on the court-house tower. It is dull silver in the moonlight. White child that sleeps upon the top of pines. Kabnis' mind clears. He sees himself yanked beneath that tower. He sees white minds, with indolent assumption, juggle justice and a nigger . . . Somewhere, far off in the straight line of his sight, is Augusta. Christ, how cut off from everything he is. And hours, hours north, why not say a lifetime north? Washington sleeps. Its still, peaceful streets, how desirable they are. Its people whom he had always halfway despised. New York? Impossible. It was a fiction. He had dreamed it. An impotent nostalgia grips him. It becomes intolerable. He forces himself to narrow to a cabin silhouetted on a knoll about a mile away. Peace. Negroes within it are content. They farm. They sing. They love. They sleep. Kabnis wonders if perhaps they can feel him. If perhaps he gives them bad dreams. Things are so immediate in Georgia.

Thinking that now he can go to sleep, he re-enters his room. He builds a fire in the open hearth. The room dances to the tongues of flames, and sings to the crackling and spurting of the logs. Wind comes up between the floor boards, through the black cracks of the walls.

Kabnis: Cant sleep. Light a cigarette. If that old bastard comes over here and smells smoke, I'm done for. Hell of a note, cant even smoke. The stillness of it: where they burn and hang men, you cant smoke. Cant take a swig of licker. What do they think this is, anyway, some sort of temperance school? How did I ever land in such a hole? Ugh. One might just as well be in his grave. Still as a grave. Jesus, how still everything is. Does the world know how still it is? People make noise. They are afraid of silence. Of what lives, and God, of what dies in silence. There must be many dead things moving in silence. They come here to touch me. I swear I feel their fingers . . . Come, Ralph, pull yourself together. What in hell was that? Only the rustle of leaves, I guess. You know, Ralph, old man, it wouldnt surprise me at all to see a ghost. People dont think there are such things. They rationalize their fear, and call their cowardice science. Fine bunch, they are. Damit, that was a noise. And not the wind either. A chicken maybe. Hell, chickens dont wander around this time of night. What in hell is it?

A scraping sound, like a piece of wood dragging over the ground, is coming near.

"Ha, ha. The ghosts down this way havent got any chains to rattle, so they drag trees along with them. Thats a good one. But no joke, something is outside this house, as sure as hell. Whatever it is, it can get a good look at me and I cant see it. Jesus Christ!"

Kabnis pours water on the flames and blows his lamp out. He picks up a poker and stealthily approaches the outside door. Swings it open, and lurches into the night. A calf, carrying a yoke of wood, bolts away from him and scampers down the road.

"Well, I'm damned. This godam place is sure getting the best of me. Come, Ralph, old man, pull yourself together. Nights cant last forever. Thank God for that. Its Sunday already. First time in my life I've ever wanted Sunday to come. Hell of a day. And down here there's no such thing as ducking church. Well, I'll see Halsey and Layman, and get a good square meal. Thats something. And Halsey's a damn good feller. Cant talk to him, though. Who in Christ's world can I talk to? A hen. God. Myself . . . I'm going bats, no doubt of that. Come now, Ralph, go in and make yourself go to sleep.

Come now . . in the door . . thats right. Put the poker down.
There. All right. Slip under the sheets. Close your eyes.
Think nothing . . a long time . . nothing, nothing. Dont
even think nothing. Blank. Not even blank. Count. No,
mustnt count. Nothing . . blank . . nothing . . blank . . space
without stars in it. No, nothing . . nothing . .

Kabnis sleeps. The winds, like soft-voiced vagrant poets sing:

> White-man's land.
> Niggers, sing.
> Burn, bear black children
> Till poor rivers bring
> Rest, and sweet glory
> In Camp Ground.

2

The parlor of Fred Halsey's home. There is a seediness about
it. It seems as though the fittings have given a frugal service to
at least seven generations of middle-class shop-owners. An
open grate burns cheerily in contrast to the gray cold changed
autumn weather. An old-fashioned mantelpiece supports a
family clock (not running), a figure or two in imitation bronze,
and two small group pictures. Directly above it, in a heavy
oak frame, the portrait of a bearded man. Black hair, thick
and curly, intensifies the pallor of the high forehead. The eyes
are daring. The nose, sharp and regular. The poise suggests a
tendency to adventure checked by the necessities of absolute
command. The portrait is that of an English gentleman who
has retained much of his culture, in that money has enabled
him to escape being drawn through a land-grubbing pioneer
life. His nature and features, modified by marriage and

circumstances, have been transmitted to his great-grandson, Fred. To the left of this picture, spaced on the wall, is a smaller portrait of the great-grandmother. That here there is a Negro strain, no one would doubt. But it is difficult to say in precisely what feature it lies. On close inspection, her mouth is seen to be wistfully twisted. The expression of her face seems to shift before one's gaze—now ugly, repulsive; now sad, and somehow beautiful in its pain. A tin woodbox rests on the floor below. To the right of the great-grandfather's portrait hangs a family group: the father, mother, two brothers, and one sister of Fred. It includes himself some thirty years ago when his face was an olive white, and his hair luxuriant and dark and wavy. The father is a rich brown. The mother, practically white. Of the children, the girl, quite young, is like Fred; the two brothers, darker. The walls of the room are plastered and painted green. An old upright piano is tucked into the corner near the window. The window looks out on a forlorn, box-like, whitewashed frame church. Negroes are gathering, on foot, driving questionable gray and brown mules, and in an occasional Ford, for afternoon service. Beyond, Georgia hills roll off into the distance, their dreary aspect heightened by the gray spots of unpainted one- and two-room shanties. Clumps of pine trees here and there are the dark points the whole landscape is approaching. The church bell tolls. Above its squat tower, a great spiral of buzzards reaches far into the heavens. An ironic comment upon the path that leads into the Christian land . . . Three rocking chairs are grouped around the grate. Sunday papers scattered on the floor indicate a recent usage. Halsey, a well-built, stocky fellow, hair cropped close, enters the room. His Sunday clothes smell of wood and glue, for it is his habit to potter around his wagon-shop even on the Lord's day. He is followed by Professor Layman, tall, heavy, loose-jointed Georgia Negro, by turns teacher and preacher, who has traveled in almost every nook and corner of the state and hence knows more than would be good for anyone other than a silent man. Kabnis, trying to force through a gathering heaviness, trails in behind them. They slip into chairs before the fire.

Layman: Sholy fine, Mr. Halsey, sholy fine. This town's right good at feedin folks, better'n most towns in th state, even for preachers, but I ken say this beats um all. Yassur. Now aint that right, Professor Kabnis?

Kabnis: Yes sir, this beats them all, all right—best I've had, and thats a fact, though my comparison doesnt carry far, y'know.

Layman: Hows that, Professor?

Kabnis: Well, this is my first time out—

Layman: For a fact. Aint seed you round so much. Whats th trouble? Dont like our folks down this away?

Halsey: Aint that, Layman. He aint like most northern niggers that way. Aint a thing stuck up about him. He likes us, you an me, maybe all—its that red mud over yonder— gets stuck in it an cant get out. (Laughs.) An then he loves th fire so, warm as its been. Coldest Yankee I've ever seen. But I'm goin t get him out now in a jiffy, eh, Kabnis?

Kabnis: Sure, I should say so, sure. Dont think its because I dont like folks down this way. Just the opposite, in fact. Theres more hospitality and everything. Its diff—that is, theres lots of northern exaggeration about the South. Its not half the terror they picture it. Things are not half bad, as one could easily figure out for himself without ever crossing the Mason and Dixie line:[5] all these people wouldnt stay down here, especially the rich, the ones that could easily leave, if conditions were so mighty bad. And then too, sometime back, my family were southerners y'know. From Georgia, in fact—

Layman: Nothin t feel proud about, Professor. Neither your folks nor mine.

Halsey (in a mock religious tone): Amen t that, brother Layman. Amen (turning to Kabnis, half playful, yet somehow dead in earnest). An Mr. Kabnis, kindly remember youre in th land of cotton—hell of a land. Th white folks get th boll; th niggers get th stalk. An dont you dare touch th boll, or even look at it. They'll swing y sho. (Laughs.)

Kabnis: But they wouldnt touch a gentleman—fellows, men like us three here—

Layman: Nigger's a nigger down this away, Professor. An only two dividins: good an bad. An even they aint permanent categories. They sometimes mixes um up when it comes t lynchin. I've seen um do it.

Halsey: Dont let th fear int y, though, Kabnis. This county's a good un. Aint been a stringin up I can remember. (Laughs.)

Layman: This is a good town an a good county. But theres some that makes up fer it.

Kabnis: Things are better now though since that stir about those peonage cases,[6] arent they?

Layman: Ever hear tell of a single shot killin moren one rabbit, Professor?

Kabnis: No, of course not, that is, but then—

Halsey: Now I know you werent born yesterday, sprung up so rapid like you aint heard of th brick thrown in th hornets' nest. (Laughs.)

Kabnis: Hardly, hardly, I know—

Halsey: Course y do. (To Layman) See, northern niggers aint as dumb as they make out t be.

Kabnis (overlooking the remark): Just stirs them up to sting.

Halsey: T perfection. An put just like a professor should put it.

Kabnis: Thats what actually did happen?

Layman: Well, if it aint sos only because th stingers already movin jes as fast as they ken go. An been goin ever since I ken remember, an then some mo. Though I dont usually make mention of it.

Halsey: Damn sight better not. Say, Layman, you come from where theyre always swarmin, dont y?

Layman: Yassur. I do that, sho. Dont want t mention it, but its a fact. I've seed th time when there werent no use t even stretch out flat upon th ground. Seen um shoot an cut a man t pieces who had died th night befo. Yassur. An they didnt stop when they found out he was dead—jes went on ahackin at him anyway.

Kabnis: What did you do? What did you say to them, Professor?

Layman: Thems th things you neither does a thing or talks about if y want t stay around this away, Professor.

Halsey: Listen t what he's tellin y, Kabnis. May come in handy some day.

Kabnis: Cant something be done? But of course not. This preacher-ridden race. Pray and shout. Theyre in the preacher's hands. Thats what it is. And the preacher's hands are in the white man's pockets.

Halsey: Present company always excepted.

Kabnis: The Professor knows I wasnt referring to him.

Layman: Preacher's a preacher anywheres you turn. No use exceptin.

Kabnis: Well, of course, if you look at it that way. I didnt mean— But cant something be done?

Layman: Sho. Yassur. An done first rate an well. Jes like Sam Raymon done it.

Kabnis: Hows that? What did he do?

Layman: Th white folks (reckon I oughtnt tell it) had jes knocked two others like you kill a cow—brained um with an ax, when they caught Sam Raymon by a stream. They was about t do fer him when he up an says, "White folks, I gotter die, I knows that. But wont y let me die in my own way?" Some was fer gettin after him, but th boss held um back an says, "Jes so longs th nigger dies—". An Sam fell down ont his knees an prayed, "O Lord, Ise comin to y," an he up an jumps int th stream.

Singing from the church becomes audible. Above it, rising and falling in a plaintive moan, a woman's voice swells to shouting. Kabnis hears it. His face gives way to an expression of mingled fear, contempt, and pity. Layman takes no notice of it. Halsey grins at Kabnis. He feels like having a little sport with him.

Halsey: Lets go t church, eh, Kabnis?

Kabnis (seeking control): All right—no sir, not by a damn sight. Once a days enough for me. Christ, but that stuff gets to me. Meaning no reflection on you, Professor.

Halsey: Course not. Say, Kabnis, noticed y this morning. What'd y get up for an go out?

Kabnis: Couldnt stand the shouting, and thats a fact. We dont have that sort of thing up North. We do, but, that is, some one should see to it that they are stopped or put out when they get so bad the preacher has to stop his sermon for them.

Halsey: Is that th way youall sit on sisters up North?

Kabnis: In the church I used to go to no one ever shouted—

Halsey: Lungs weak?

Kabnis: Hardly, that is—

Halsey: Yankees are right up t th minute in tellin folk how t turn a trick. They always were good at talkin.

Kabnis: Well, anyway, they should be stopped.

Layman: Thats right. Thats true. An its th worst ones in th community that comes int th church t shout. I've sort a made a study of it. You take a man what drinks, th biggest lickerhead around will come int th church an yell th loudest. An th sister whats done wrong, an is always doin wrong, will sit down in th Amen corner[7] an swing her arms an shout her head off. Seems as if they cant control themselves out in th world; they cant control themselves in church. Now dont that sound logical, Professor?

Halsey: Reckon its as good as any. But I heard that queer cuss over yonder—y know him, dont y, Kabnis? Well, y ought t. He had a run-in with your boss th other day—same as you'll have if you dont walk th chalk-line. An th quicker th better. I hate that Hanby. Ornery bastard. I'll mash his mouth in one of these days. Well, as I was sayin, that feller, Lewis's name, I heard him sayin somethin about a stream whats dammed has got t cut loose somewheres. An that sounds good. I know th feelin myself. He strikes me as knowin a bucketful bout most things, that feller does. Seems like he doesnt want t talk, an does, sometimes, like Layman here. Damn queer feller, him.

Layman: Cant make heads or tails of him, an I've seen lots o queer possums in my day. Everybody's wonderin about him. White folks too. He'll have t leave here soon, thats sho. Always askin questions. An I aint seed his lips move once. Pokin round an notin somethin. Noted what I said th other day, an that werent fer notin down.

Kabnis: What was that?

Layman: Oh, a lynchin that took place bout a year ago. Th worst I know of round these parts.

Halsey: Bill Burnam?

Layman: Na. Mame Lamkins.

Halsey grunts, but says nothing.

The preacher's voice rolls from the church in an insistent chanting monotone. At regular intervals it rises to a crescendo note. The sister begins to shout. Her voice, high-pitched and hysterical, is almost perfectly attuned to the nervous key of Kabnis. Halsey notices his distress, and is amused by it. Layman's face is expressionless. Kabnis wants to hear the story of Mame Lamkins. He does not want to hear it. It can be no worse than the shouting.

Kabnis (his chair rocking faster): What about Mame Lamkins?

Halsey: Tell him, Layman.

The preacher momentarily stops. The choir, together with the entire congregation, sings an old spiritual. The music seems to quiet the shouter. Her heavy breathing has the sound of evening winds that blow through pinecones. Layman's voice is uniformly low and soothing. A canebrake, murmuring the tale to its neighbor-road would be more passionate.

Layman: White folks know that niggers talk, an they dont mind jes so long as nothing comes of it, so here goes. She was in th family-way, Mame Lamkins was. They killed her in th street, an some white man seein th risin in her stomach as she lay there soppy in her blood like any cow, took an ripped her belly open, an th kid fell out. It was living; but a nigger baby aint supposed t live. So he jabbed his knife in it an stuck it t a tree. An then they all went away.[8]

Kabnis: Christ no! What had she done?

Layman: Tried t hide her husband when they was after him.

A shriek pierces the room. The bronze pieces on the mantel hum. The sister cries frantically: "Jesus, Jesus, I've found Jesus. O Lord, glory t God, one mo sinner is acomin home." At the height of this, a stone, wrapped round with paper, crashes through the window. Kabnis springs to his feet, terror-stricken. Layman is worried. Halsey picks up the stone. Takes off the wrapper, smooths it out, and reads: "You northern nigger, its time fer y t leave. Git along now." Kabnis knows that the command is meant for him. Fear squeezes him. Caves him in. As a violent external pressure would. Fear flows inside him. It fills him up. He bloats. He saves himself from bursting by dashing wildly from the room. Halsey and Layman stare stupidly at each other. The stone, the crumpled paper are things, huge things that weight them. Their thoughts are vaguely concerned with the texture of the stone, with the color of the paper. Then they remember the words, and begin to shift them about in sentences. Layman even construes them grammatically. Suddenly the sense of them comes back to Halsey. He grips Layman by the arm and they both follow after Kabnis.

A false dusk has come early. The country-side is ashen, chill. Cabins and roads and canebrakes whisper. The church choir, dipping into a long silence, sings:

> My Lord, what a mourning,
> My Lord, what a mourning,
> My Lord, what a mourning,
> When the stars begin to fall.[9]

Softly luminous over the hills and valleys, the faint spray of a scattered star . . .

3

A splotchy figure drives forward along the cane- and corn-stalk hemmed-in road. A scarecrow replica of Kabnis, awkwardly animate. Fantastically plastered with red Georgia mud. It skirts the big house whose windows shine like mellow lanterns in the dusk. Its shoulder jogs against a sweet-gum tree. The figure caroms off against the cabin door, and lunges in. It slams the door as if to prevent some one entering after it.

"God Almighty, theyre here. After me. On me. All along the road I saw their eyes flaring from the cane. Hounds. Shouts.

What in God's name did I run here for? A mud-hole trap. I stumbled on a rope. O God, a rope. Their clammy hands were like the love of death playing up and down my spine. Trying to trip my legs. To trip my spine. Up and down my spine. My spine . . . My legs . . . Why in hell didn't they catch me?"

Kabnis wheels around, half defiant, half numbed with a more immediate fear.

"Wanted to trap me here. Get out o there. I see you."

He grabs a broom from beside the chimney and violently pokes it under the bed. The broom strikes a tin wash-tub. The noise bewilders. He recovers.

"Not there. In the closet."

He throws the broom aside and grips the poker. Starts towards the closet door, towards somewhere in the perfect blackness behind the chimney.

"I'll brain you."

He stops short. The barks of hounds, evidently in pursuit, reach him. A voice, liquid in distance, yells, "Hi! Hi!"

"O God, theyre after me. Holy Father, Mother of Christ— hell, this aint no time for prayer—"

Voices, just outside the door:

"Reckon he's here."

"Dont see no light though."

The door is flung open.

Kabnis: Get back or I'll kill you.

He braces himself, brandishing the poker.

Halsey (coming in): Aint as bad as all that. Put that thing down.

Layman: Its only us, Professor. Nobody else after y.

Kabnis: Halsey. Layman. Close that door. Dont light that light. For godsake get away from there.

Halsey: Nobody's after y, Kabnis, I'm tellin y. Put that thing down an get yourself together.

Kabnis: I tell you they are. I saw them. I heard the hounds.

Halsey: These aint th days of hounds an Uncle Tom's Cabin, feller. White folks aint in fer all them theatrics these days. Theys more direct than that. If what they wanted was t get y, theyd have just marched right in an took y where y sat. Somebodys down by th branch chasin rabbits an atreein possums.

A shot is heard.

Halsey: Got him, I reckon. Saw Tom goin out with his gun. Tom's pretty lucky most times.

He goes to the bureau and lights the lamp. The circular fringe is patterned on the ceiling. The moving shadows of the men are huge against the bare wall boards. Halsey walks up to Kabnis, takes the poker from his grip, and without more ado pushes him into a chair before the dark hearth.

Halsey: Youre a mess. Here, Layman. Get some trash an start a fire.

Layman fumbles around, finds some newspapers and old bags, puts them in the hearth, arranges the wood, and kindles the fire. Halsey sets a black iron kettle where it soon will be boiling. Then takes from his hip-pocket a bottle of corn licker which he passes to Kabnis.

Halsey: Here. This'll straighten y out a bit.

Kabnis nervously draws the cork and gulps the licker down.

Kabnis: Ha. Good stuff. Thanks. Thank y, Halsey.

Halsey: Good stuff! Youre damn right. Hanby there dont think so. Wonder he doesnt come over t find out whos burnin his oil. Miserly bastard, him. Th boys what made this stuff— are y listenin t me, Kabnis? th boys what made this stuff have got th art down like I heard you say youd like t be with words. Eh? Have some, Layman?

Layman: Dont think I care for none, thank y jes th same, Mr. Halsey.

Halsey: Care hell. Course y care. Everybody cares around

these parts. Preachers an school teachers an everybody. Here.
Here, take it. Dont try that line on me.

Layman limbers up a little, but he cannot quite forget that
he is on school ground.

Layman: Thats right. Thats true, sho. Shinin is th only
business what pays in these hard times.[10]

He takes a nip, and passes the bottle to Kabnis. Kabnis is
in the middle of a long swig when a rap sounds on the door.
He almost spills the bottle, but manages to pass it to Halsey
just as the door swings open and Hanby enters. He is a well-
dressed, smooth, rich, black-skinned Negro who thinks
there is no one quite so suave and polished as himself. To
members of his own race, he affects the manners of a wealthy
white planter. Or, when he is up North, he lets it be known
that his ideas are those of the best New England tradition.
To white men he bows, without ever completely humbling
himself. Tradesmen in the town tolerate him because he
spends his money with them. He delivers his words with a
full consciousness of his moral superiority.

Hanby: Hum. Erer, Professor Kabnis, to come straight to
the point: the progress of the Negro race is jeopardized
whenever the personal habits and examples set by its guides
and mentors fall below the acknowledged and hard-won
standard of its average member. This institution, of which I
am the humble president, was founded, and has been maintained at a cost of great labor and untold sacrifice. Its purpose is to teach our youth to live better, cleaner, more noble
lives. To prove to the world that the Negro race can be just
like any other race. It hopes to attain this aim partly by the
salutary examples set by its instructors. I cannot hinder the
progress of a race simply to indulge a single member. I have
thought the matter out beforehand, I can assure you. Therefore, if I find your resignation on my desk by to-morrow

morning, Mr. Kabnis, I shall not feel obliged to call in the sheriff. Otherwise . . .

Kabnis: A fellow can take a drink in his own room if he wants to, in the privacy of his own room.

Hanby: His room, but not the institution's room, Mr. Kabnis.

Kabnis: This is my room while I'm in it.

Hanby: Mr. Clayborn (the sheriff) can inform you as to that.

Kabnis: Oh, well, what do I care—glad to get out of this mud-hole.

Hanby: I should think so from your looks.

Kabnis: You neednt get sarcastic about it.

Hanby: No, that is true. And I neednt wait for your resignation either, Mr. Kabnis.

Kabnis: Oh, you'll get that all right. Dont worry.

Hanby: And I should like to have the room thoroughly aired and cleaned and ready for your successor by to-morrow noon, Professor.

Kabnis (trying to rise): You can have your godam room right away. I dont want it.

Hanby: But I wont have your cursing.

Halsey pushes Kabnis back into his chair.

Halsey: Sit down, Kabnis, till I wash y.

Hanby (to Halsey): I would rather not have drinking men on the premises, Mr. Halsey. You will oblige me—

Halsey: I'll oblige you by stayin right on this spot, this spot, get me? till I get damned ready t leave.

He approaches Hanby. Hanby retreats, but manages to hold his dignity.

Halsey: Let me get you told right now, Mr. Samuel Hanby. Now listen t me. I aint no slick an span slave youve hired, an dont y think it for a minute. Youve bullied enough about this town. An besides, wheres that bill youve been owin me?

Listen t me. If I dont get it paid in by tmorrer noon, Mr. Hanby (he mockingly assumes Hanby's tone and manner), I shall feel obliged t call th sheriff. An that sheriff'll be myself who'll catch y in th road an pull y out your buggy an rightly attend t y. You heard me. Now leave him alone. I'm takin him home with me. I got it fixed. Before you came in. He's goin t work with me. Shapin shafts and buildin wagons'll make a man of him what nobody, y get me? what nobody can take advantage of. Thats all . . .

Halsey burrs off into vague and incoherent comment.

Pause. Disagreeable.

Layman's eyes are glazed on the spurting fire.

Kabnis wants to rise and put both Halsey and Hanby in their places. He vaguely knows that he must do this, else the power of direction will completely slip from him to those outside. The conviction is just strong enough to torture him. To bring a feverish, quick-passing flare into his eyes. To mutter words soggy in hot saliva. To jerk his arms upward in futile protest. Halsey, noticing his gestures, thinks it is water that he desires. He brings a glass to him. Kabnis slings it to the floor. Heat of the conviction dies. His arms crumple. His upper lip, his mustache, quiver. Rap! rap, on the door. The sounds slap Kabnis. They bring a hectic color to his cheeks. Like huge cold finger tips they touch his skin and goose-flesh it. Hanby strikes a commanding pose. He moves toward Layman. Layman's face is innocently immobile.

Halsey: Whos there?

Voice: Lewis.

Halsey: Come in, Lewis. Come on in.

Lewis enters. He is the queer fellow who has been referred to. A tall wiry copper-colored man, thirty perhaps. His mouth and eyes suggest purpose guided by an adequate intelligence. He is what a stronger Kabnis might have been, and in an odd faint way resembles him. As he steps towards the others, he seems to be issuing sharply from a vivid dream. Lewis shakes hands with Halsey. Nods perfunctorily to Hanby, who has stiffened to meet him. Smiles rapidly at Layman, and settles with real interest on Kabnis.

Lewis: Kabnis passed me on the road. Had a piece of business of my own, and couldnt get here any sooner. Thought I might be able to help in some way or other.

Halsey: A good baths bout all he needs now. An somethin t put his mind t rest.

Lewis: I think I can give him that. That note was meant for me. Some Negroes have grown uncomfortable at my being here—

Kabnis: You mean, Mr. Lewis, some colored folks threw it? Christ Amighty!

Halsey: Thats what he means. An just as I told y. White folks more direct than that.

Kabnis: What are they after you for?

Lewis: Its a long story, Kabnis. Too long for now. And it might involve present company. (He laughs pleasantly and gestures vaguely in the direction of Hanby.) Tell you about it later on perhaps.

Kabnis: Youre not going?

Lewis: Not till my month's up.

Halsey: Hows that?

Lewis: I'm on a sort of contract with myself. (Is about to leave.) Well, glad its nothing serious—

Halsey: Come round t th shop sometime why dont y, Lewis? I've asked y enough. I'd like t have a talk with y. I aint as dumb as I look. Kabnis an me'll be in most any time. Not much work these days. Wish t hell there was. This burg gets to me when there aint. (In answer to Lewis' question.) He's goin t work with me. Ya. Night air this side th branch aint good fer him. (Looks at Hanby. Laughs.)

Lewis: I see . . .

His eyes turn to Kabnis. In the instant of their shifting, a vision of the life they are to meet. Kabnis, a promise of a soil-soaked beauty; uprooted, thinning out. Suspended a few feet above the soil whose touch would resurrect him. Arm's length removed from him whose will to help . . . There is a swift intuitive interchange of consciousness. Kabnis has a sudden need to rush into the arms of this man. His eyes call, "Brother." And then a savage, cynical twist-about within him mocks his impulse and strengthens him to repulse Lewis. His lips curl cruelly. His eyes laugh. They are glittering needles, stitching. With a throbbing ache they draw Lewis to. Lewis brusquely wheels on Hanby.

Lewis: I'd like to see you, sir, a moment, if you dont mind.

Hanby's tight collar and vest effectively preserve him.

Hanby: Yes, erer, Mr. Lewis. Right away.

Lewis: See you later, Halsey.

Halsey: So long—thanks—sho hope so, Lewis.

As he opens the door and Hanby passes out, a woman, miles down the valley, begins to sing. Her song is a spark that travels swiftly to the near-by cabins. Like purple tallow flames, songs jet up. They spread a ruddy haze over the heavens. The haze swings low. Now the whole countryside is a soft chorus. Lord. O Lord . . . Lewis closes the door behind him. A flame jets out . . .

The kettle is boiling. Halsey notices it. He pulls the wash-tub from beneath the bed. He arranges for the bath before the fire.

Halsey: Told y them theatrics didnt fit a white man. Th niggers, just like I told y. An after him. Aint surprisin though.

He aint bowed t none of them. Nassur. T nairy a one of them
nairy an inch nairy a time. An only mixed when he was good
an ready—

Kabnis: That song, Halsey, do you hear it?

Halsey: Thats a man. Hear me, Kabnis? A man—

Kabnis: Jesus, do you hear it.

Halsey: Hear it? Hear what? Course I hear it. Listen t
what I'm tellin y. A man, get me? They'll get him yet if he
dont watch out.

Kabnis is jolted into his fear.

Kabnis: Get him? What do you mean? How? Not
lynch him?

Halsey: Na. Take a shotgun an shoot his eyes clear out.
Well, anyway, it wasnt fer you, just like I told y. You'll stay
over at th house an work with me, eh, boy? Good t get away
from his nobs, eh? Damn big stiff though, him. An youre not
th first an I can tell y. (Laughs.)

He bustles and fusses about Kabnis as if he were a child.
Kabnis submits, wearily. He has no will to resist him.

Layman (his voice is like a deep hollow echo): Thats right.
Thats true, sho. Everybody's been expectin that th bust up
was comin. Surprised um all y held on as long as y did.
Teachin in th South aint th thing fer y. Nassur. You ought t
be way back up North where sometimes I wish I was. But
I've hung on down this away so long—

Halsey: An there'll never be no leavin time fer y.

4

A month has passed.

Halsey's workshop. It is an old building just off the main
street of Sempter. The walls to within a few feet of the

ground are of an age-worn cement mixture. On the outside they are considerably crumbled and peppered with what looks like musket-shot. Inside, the plaster has fallen away in great chunks, leaving the laths, grayed and cobwebbed, exposed. A sort of loft above the shop proper serves as a breakwater for the rain and sunshine which otherwise would have free entry to the main floor. The shop is filled with old wheels and parts of wheels, broken shafts, and wooden litter. A double door, midway the street wall. To the left of this, a work-bench that holds a vise and a variety of wood-work tools. A window with as many panes broken as whole, throws light on the bench. Opposite, in the rear wall, a second window looks out upon the back yard. In the left wall, a rickety smoke-blackened chimney, and hearth with fire blazing. Smooth-worn chairs grouped about the hearth suggest the village meeting-place. Several large wooden blocks, chipped and cut and sawed on their upper surfaces are in the middle of the floor. They are the supports used in almost any sort of wagon-work. Their idleness means that Halsey has no worth-while job on foot. To the right of the central door is a junk heap, and directly behind this, stairs that lead down into the cellar. The cellar is known as "The Hole." Besides being the home of a very old man, it is used by Halsey on those occasions when he spices up the life of the small town.

Halsey, wonderfully himself in his work overalls, stands in the doorway and gazes up the street, expectantly. Then his eyes grow listless. He slouches against the smooth-rubbed frame. He lights a cigarette. Shifts his position. Braces an arm against the door. Kabnis passes the window and stoops to get in under Halsey's arm. He is awkward and ludicrous, like a schoolboy in his big brother's new overalls. He skirts the large blocks on the floor, and drops into a chair before the fire. Halsey saunters towards him.

Kabnis: Time f lunch.

Halsey: Ya.

He stands by the hearth, rocking backward and forward. He stretches his hands out to the fire. He washes them in the warm glow of the flames. They never get cold, but he warms them.

Kabnis: Saw Lewis up th street. Said he'd be down.

Halsey's eyes brighten. He looks at Kabnis. Turns away. Says nothing. Kabnis fidgets. Twists his thin blue cloth-covered limbs. Pulls closer to the fire till the heat stings his shins. Pushes back. Pokes the burned logs. Puts on several fresh ones. Fidgets. The town bell strikes twelve.

Kabnis: Fix it up f tnight?

Halsey: Leave it t me.

Kabnis: Get Lewis in?

Halsey: Tryin t.

The air is heavy with the smell of pine and resin. Green logs spurt and sizzle. Sap trickles from an old pine-knot into the flames. Layman enters. He carries a lunch-pail. Kabnis, for the moment, thinks that he is a day laborer.

Layman: Evenin, gen'lemun.

Both: Whats say, Layman.

Layman squares a chair to the fire and droops into it. Several town fellows, silent unfathomable men for the most part, saunter in. Overalls. Thick tan shoes. Felt hats marvelously shaped and twisted. One asks Halsey for a cigarette. He gets it. The blacksmith, a tremendous black man, comes in from the forge. Not even a nod from him. He picks up an axle and goes out. Lewis enters. The town men look curiously at him. Suspicion and an open liking contest for possession of their faces. They are uncomfortable. One by one they drift into the street.

Layman: Heard y was leavin, Mr. Lewis.

Kabnis: Months up, eh? Hell of a month I've got.

Halsey: Sorry y goin, Lewis. Just getting acquainted like.

Lewis: Sorry myself, Halsey, in a way—

Layman: Gettin t like our town, Mr. Lewis?

Lewis: I'm afraid its on a different basis, Professor.

Halsey: An I've yet t hear about that basis. Been waitin long enough, God knows. Seems t me like youd take pity on a feller if nothin more.

Kabnis: Somethin that old black cockroach over yonder doesnt like, whatever it is.

Layman: Thats right. Thats right, sho.

Halsey: A feller dropped in here tother day an said he knew what you was about. Said you had queer opinions. Well, I could have told him you was a queer one, myself. But not th way he was driftin. Didnt mean anything by it, but just let drop he thought you was a little wrong up here— crazy, y'know. (Laughs.)

Kabnis: Y mean old Blodson? Hell, he's bats himself.

Lewis: I remember him. We had a talk. But what he found queer, I think, was not my opinions, but my lack of them. In half an hour he had settled everything: boll weevils, God, the World War. Weevils and wars are the pests that God sends against the sinful. People are too weak to correct themselves: the Redeemer is coming back. Get ready, ye sinners, for the advent of Our Lord. Interesting, eh, Kabnis? but not exactly what we want.

Halsey: Y could have come t me. I've sho been after y enough. Most every time I've seen y.

Kabnis (sarcastically): Hows it y never came t us professors?

Lewis: I did—to one.

Kabnis: Y mean t say y got somethin from that celluloid-collar-eraser-cleaned old codger over in th mud hole?

Halsey: Rough on th old boy, aint he? (Laughs.)

Lewis: Something, yes. Layman here could have given me

quite a deal, but the incentive to his keeping quiet is so much greater than anything I could have offered him to open up, that I crossed him off my mind. And you—

Kabnis: What about me?

Halsey: Tell him, Lewis, for godsake tell him. I've told him. But its somethin else he wants so bad I've heard him downstairs mumblin with th old man.

Lewis: The old man?

Kabnis: What about me? Come on now, you know so much.

Halsey: Tell him, Lewis. Tell it t him.

Lewis: Life has already told him more than he is capable of knowing. It has given him in excess of what he can receive. I have been offered. Stuff in his stomach curdled, and he vomited me.

Kabnis' face twitches. His body writhes.

Kabnis: You know a lot, you do. How about Halsey?

Lewis: Yes . . . Halsey? Fits here. Belongs here. An artist in your way, arent you, Halsey?

Halsey: Reckon I am, Lewis. Give me th work and fair pay an I aint askin nothin better. Went over-seas an saw France; an I come back. Been up North; an I come back. Went t school; but there aint no books whats got th feel t them of them there tools. Nassur. An I'm atellin y.

A shriveled, bony white man passes the window and enters the shop. He carries a broken hatchet-handle and the severed head. He speaks with a flat, drawn voice to Halsey, who comes forward to meet him.

Mr. Ramsay: Can y fix this fer me, Halsey?

Halsey (looking it over): Reckon so, Mr. Ramsay. Here, Kabnis. A little practice fer y.

Halsey directs Kabnis, showing him how to place the handle in the vise, and cut it down. The knife hangs. Kabnis thinks that it must be dull. He jerks it hard. The tool goes deep and shaves too much off. Mr. Ramsay smiles brokenly at him.

Mr. Ramsay (to Halsey): Still breakin in the new hand, eh, Halsey? Seems like a likely enough faller once he gets th hang of it.

He gives a tight laugh at his own good humor. Kabnis burns red. The back of his neck stings him beneath his collar. He feels stifled. Through Ramsay, the whole white South weighs down upon him. The pressure is terrific. He sweats under the arms. Chill beads run down his body. His brows concentrate upon the handle as though his own life was staked upon the perfect shaving of it. He begins to out and out botch the job. Halsey smiles.

Halsey: He'll make a good un some of these days, Mr. Ramsay.

Mr. Ramsay: Y ought t know. Yer daddy was a good un before y. Runs in th family, seems like t me.

Halsey: Thats right, Mr. Ramsay.

Kabnis is hopeless. Halsey takes the handle from him. With a few deft strokes he shaves it. Fits it. Gives it to Ramsay.

Mr. Ramsay: How much on this?

Halsey: No charge, Mr. Ramsay.

Mr. Ramsay (going out): All right, Halsey. Come down an take it out in trade. Shoe-strings or something.

Halsey: Yassur, Mr. Ramsay.

Halsey rejoins Lewis and Layman. Kabnis, hangdog-fashion, follows him.

Halsey: They like y if y work fer them.

Layman: Thats right, Mr. Halsey. Thats right, sho.

The group is about to resume its talk when Hanby enters. He is all energy, bustle, and business. He goes direct to Kabnis.

Hanby: An axle is out in the buggy which I would like to have shaped into a crow-bar. You will see that it is fixed for me.

Without waiting for an answer, and knowing that Kabnis will follow, he passes out. Kabnis, scowling, silent, trudges after him.

Hanby (from the outside): I lave that ready for me by three o'clock, young man. I shall call for it.

Kabnis (under his breath as he comes in): Th hell you say, you old black swamp-gut.

He slings the axle on the floor.

Halsey: Wheeee!

Layman, lunch finished long ago, rises, heavily. He shakes hands with Lewis.

Layman: Might not see y again befo y leave, Mr. Lewis. I enjoys t hear y talk. Y might have been a preacher. Maybe a bishop some day. Sho do hope t see y back this away again sometime, Mr. Lewis.

Lewis: Thanks, Professor. Hope I'll see you.

Layman waves a long arm loosely to the others, and leaves. Kabnis goes to the door. His eyes, sullen, gaze up the street.

Kabnis: Carrie K.'s comin with th lunch. Bout time.

She passes the window. Her red girl's-cap, catching the sun, flashes vividly. With a stiff, awkward little movement she crosses the door-sill and gives Kabnis one of the two baskets which she is carrying. There is a slight stoop to her shoulders. The curves of her body blend with this to a soft rounded charm. Her gestures are stiffly variant. Black bangs curl over the forehead of her oval-olive face. Her expression is dazed, but on provocation it can melt into a wistful smile. Adolescent. She is easily the sister of Fred Halsey.

Carrie K.: Mother says excuse her, brother Fred an Ralph, fer bein late.

Kabnis: Everythings all right an O.K., Carrie Kate. O.K. an all right.

The two men settle on their lunch. Carrie, with hardly a glance in the direction of the hearth, as is her habit, is about to take the second basket down to the old man, when Lewis rises. In doing so he draws her unwitting attention. Their meeting is a swift sun-burst. Lewis impulsively moves towards her. His mind flashes images of her life in the southern town. He sees the nascent woman, her flesh already stiffening to cartilage, drying to bone. Her spirit-bloom, even now touched sullen, bitter. Her rich beauty fading . . . He wants to— He stretches forth his hands to hers. He takes them. They feel like warm cheeks against his palms. The sun-burst from her eyes floods up and haloes him. Christ-eyes, his eyes look to her. Fearlessly she loves into them. And then something happens. Her face blanches. Awkwardly she draws away. The sin-bogies of respectable southern colored folks clamor at her: "Look out! Be a *good* girl. A *good* girl. Look out!" She gropes for her basket that has fallen to the floor. Finds it, and marches with a rigid gravity to her task of feeding the old man. Like the glowing white ash of burned paper, Lewis' eyelids, wavering, settle down. He stirs in the direction of the rear window. From the back yard, mules tethered to odd trees and posts blink dumbly at him. They too seem burdened with an impotent pain. Kabnis and Halsey are still busy with their lunch. They havent noticed him. After a while he turns to them.

Lewis: Your sister, Halsey, whats to become of her? What are you going to do for her?

Halsey: Who? What? What am I goin t do? . .

Lewis: What I mean is, what does she do down there?

Halsey: Oh. Feeds th old man. Had lunch, Lewis?

Lewis: Thanks, yes. You have never felt her, have you,

Halsey? Well, no, I guess not. I dont suppose you can. Nor
can she . . . Old man? Halsey, some one lives down there?
I've never heard of him. Tell me—

Kabnis takes time from his meal to answer with some em-
phasis:

Kabnis: Theres lots of things you aint heard of.

Lewis: Dare say. I'd like to see him.

Kabnis: You'll get all th chance you want tnight.

Halsey: Fixin a little somethin up fer tnight, Lewis. Th
three of us an some girls. Come round bout ten-thirty.

Lewis: Glad to. But what under the sun does he do down
there?

Halsey: Ask Kabnis. He blows off t him every chance he gets.

Kabnis gives a grunting laugh. His mouth twists. Carrie re-
turns from the cellar. Avoiding Lewis, she speaks to her brother.

Carrie K.: Brother Fred, father hasnt eaten now goin on th
second week, but mumbles an talks funny, or tries t talk
when I put his hands ont th food. He frightens me, an I
dunno what t do. An oh, I came near fergettin, brother, but
Mr. Marmon—he was eatin lunch when I saw him—told me
t tell y that th lumber wagon busted down an he wanted y t
fix it fer him. Said he reckoned he could get it t y after he ate.

Halsey chucks a half-eaten sandwich in the fire. Gets up. Arranges his blocks. Goes to the door and looks anxiously up the
street. The wind whirls a small spiral in the gray dust road.

Halsey: Why didnt y tell me sooner, little sister?

Carrie K.: I fergot t, an just remembered it now, brother.

Her soft rolled words are fresh pain to Lewis. He wants to
take her North with him What for? He wonders what Kabnis could do for her. What she could do for him. Mother
him. Carrie gathers the lunch things, silently, and in her
pinched manner, curtsies, and departs. Kabnis lights his
after-lunch cigarette. Lewis, who has sensed a change, becomes

aware that he is not included in it. He starts to ask again about the old man. Decides not to. Rises to go.

Lewis: Think I'll run along, Halsey.

Halsey: Sure. Glad t see y any time.

Kabnis: Dont forget tnight.

Lewis: Dont worry. I wont. So long.

Kabnis: So long. We'll be expectin y.

Lewis passes Halsey at the door. Halsey's cheeks form a vacant smile. His eyes are wide awake, watching for the wagon to turn from Broad Street into his road.

Halsey: So long.

His words reach Lewis halfway to the corner.

5

Night, soft belly of a pregnant Negress, throbs evenly against the torso of the South. Night throbs a womb-song to the South. Cane- and cotton-fields, pine forests, cypress swamps, sawmills, and factories are fecund at her touch. Night's womb-song sets them singing. Night winds are the breathing of the unborn child whose calm throbbing in the belly of a Negress sets them somnolently singing. Hear their song.

> White-man's land.
> Niggers, sing.
> Burn, bear black children
> Till poor rivers bring
> Rest, and sweet glory
> In Camp Ground.

Sempter's streets are vacant and still. White paint on the wealthier houses has the chill blue glitter of distant stars.

Negro cabins are a purple blur. Broad Street is deserted.
Winds stir beneath the corrugated iron canopies and dangle
odd bits of rope tied to horse- and mule-gnawed hitching-
posts. One store window has a light in it. Chesterfield cigarette and Chero-Cola cardboard advertisements are stacked
in it. From a side door two men come out. Pause, for a last
word and then say good night. Soon they melt in shadows
thicker than they. Way off down the street four figures sway
beneath iron awnings which form a sort of corridor that im-
perfectly echoes and jumbles what they say. A fifth form
joins them. They turn into the road that leads to Halsey's
workshop. The old building is phosphorescent above deep
shade. The figures pass through the double door. Night
winds whisper in the eaves. Sing weirdly in the ceiling cracks.
Stir curls of shavings on the floor. Halsey lights a candle. A
good-sized lumber wagon, wheels off, rests upon the blocks.
Kabnis makes a face at it. An unearthly hush is upon the
place. No one seems to want to talk. To move, lest the scraping of their feet . .

Halsey: Come on down this way, folks.

He leads the way. Stella follows. And close after her, Cora,
Lewis, and Kabnis. They descend into the Hole. It seems
huge, limitless in the candle light. The walls are of stone,
wonderfully fitted. They have no openings save a small iron-
barred window toward the top of each. They are dry and
warm. The ground slopes away to the rear of the building
and thus leaves the south wall exposed to the sun. The blacksmith's shop is plumb against the right wall. The floor is clay.
Shavings have at odd times been matted into it. In the right-
hand corner, under the stairs, two good-sized pine mattresses, resting on cardboard, are on either side of a wooden
table. On this are several half-burned candles and an oil
lamp. Behind the table, an irregular piece of mirror hangs on

the wall. A loose something that looks to be a gaudy ball costume dangles from a near-by hook. To the front, a second table holds a lamp and several whiskey glasses. Six rickety chairs are near this table. Two old wagon wheels rest on the floor. To the left, sitting in a high-backed chair which stands upon a low platform, the old man. He is like a bust in black walnut. Gray-bearded. Gray-haired. Prophetic. Immobile. Lewis' eyes are sunk in him. The others, unconcerned, are about to pass on to the front table when Lewis grips Halsey and so turns him that the candle flame shines obliquely on the old man's features.

Lewis: And he rules over—

Kabnis: Th smoke an fire of th forge.

Lewis: Black Vulcan?[11] I wouldnt say so. That forehead. Great woolly beard. Those eyes. A mute John the Baptist[12] of a new religion—or a tongue-tied shadow of an old.

Kabnis: His tongue is tied all right, an I can vouch f that.

Lewis: Has he never talked to you?

Halsey: Kabnis wont give him a chance.

He laughs. The girls laugh. Kabnis winces.

Lewis: What do you call him?

Halsey: Father.

Lewis: Good. Father what?

Kabnis: Father of hell.

Halsey: Father's th only name we have for him. Come on. Lets sit down an get t th pleasure of the evenin.

Lewis: Father John it is from now on . . .

Slave boy whom some Christian mistress taught to read the Bible. Black man who saw Jesus in the ricefields, and began preaching to his people. Moses- and Christ-words used for songs. Dead blind father of a muted folk who feel their way upward to a life that crushes or absorbs them.

(Speak, Father!) Suppose your eyes could see, old man. (The years hold hands. O Sing!) Suppose your lips . . .

Halsey, does he never talk?

Halsey: Na. But sometimes. Only seldom. Mumbles. Sis says he talks—

Kabnis: I've heard him talk.

Halsey: First I've ever heard of it. You dont give him a chance. Sis says she's made out several words, mostly one— an like as not cause it was "sin."

Kabnis: All those old fogies stutter about sin.

Cora laughs in a loose sort of way. She is a tall, thin, mulatto woman. Her eyes are deepset behind a pointed nose. Her hair is coarse and bushy. Seeing that Stella also is restless, she takes her arm and the two women move towards the table. They slip into chairs. Halsey follows and lights the lamp. He lays out a pack of cards. Stella sorts them as if telling fortunes. She is a beautifully proportioned, large-eyed, brown-skin girl. Except for the twisted line of her mouth when she smiles or laughs, there is about her no suggestion of the life she's been through. Kabnis, with great mock-solemnity, goes to the corner, takes down the robe, and dons it. He is a curious spectacle, acting a part, yet very real. He joins the others at the table. They are used to him. Lewis is surprised. He laughs. Kabnis shrinks and then glares at him with a furtive hatred. Halsey, bringing out a bottle of corn licker, pours drinks.

Halsey: Come on, Lewis. Come on, you fellers. Heres lookin at y.

Then, as if suddenly recalling something, he jerks away from the table and starts towards the steps.

Kabnis: Where y goin, Halsey?

Halsey: Where? Where y think? That oak beam in th wagon—

Kabnis: Come ere. Come ere. Sit down. What in hell's wrong with you fellers? You with your wagon. Lewis with his Father John. This aint th time fer foolin with wagons. Daytime's bad enough f that. Ere, sit down. Ere, Lewis, you too sit down. Have a drink. Thats right. Drink corn licker, love th girls, an listen t th old man mumblin sin.

There seems to be no good-time spirit to the party. Something in the air is too tense and deep for that. Lewis, seated now so that his eyes rest upon the old man, merges with his source and lets the pain and beauty of the South meet him there. White faces, pain-pollen, settle downward through a cane-sweet mist and touch the ovaries of yellow flowers. Cotton-bolls bloom, droop. Black roots twist in a parched red soil beneath a blazing sky. Magnolias, fragrant, a trifle futile, lovely, far off . . . His eyelids close. A force begins to heave and rise . . . Stella is serious, reminiscent.

Stella: Usall is brought up t hate sin worse than death—

Kabnis: An then before you have y eyes half open, youre made t love it if y want t live.

Stella: Us never—

Kabnis: Oh, I know your story: that old prim bastard over yonder, an then old Calvert's office—

Stella: It wasnt them—

Kabnis: I know. They put y out of church, an then I guess th preacher came around an asked f some. But thats your body. Now me—

Halsey (passing him the bottle): All right, kid, we believe y. Here, take another. Wheres Clover, Stel?

Stella: You know how Jim is when he's just out th swamp. Done up in shine[13] an wouldnt let her come. Said he'd bust her head open if she went out.

Kabnis: Dont see why he doesnt stay over with Laura, where he belongs.

Stella: Ask him, an I reckon he'll tell y. More than you want.

Halsey: Th nigger hates th sight of a black woman worse than death. Sorry t mix y up this way, Lewis. But y see how tis.

Lewis' skin is tight and glowing over the fine bones of his face. His lips tremble. His nostrils quiver. The others notice this and smile knowingly at each other. Drinks and smokes are passed around. They pay no neverminds to him. A real party is being worked up. Then Lewis opens his eyes and looks at them. Their smiles disperse in hot-cold tremors. Kabnis chokes his laugh. It sputters, gurgles. His eyes flicker and turn away. He tries to pass the thing off by taking a long drink which he makes considerable fuss over. He is drawn back to Lewis. Seeing Lewis' gaze still upon him, he scowls.

Kabnis: Whatsha lookin at me for? Y want t know who I am? Well, I'm Ralph Kabnis—lot of good its goin t do y. Well? Whatsha keep lookin for? I'm Ralph Kabnis. Aint that enough f y? Want th whole family history? Its none of your godam business, anyway. Keep off me. Do y hear? Keep off me. Look at Cora. Aint she pretty enough t look at? Look at Halsey, or Stella. Clover ought t be here an you could look at her. An love her. Thats what you need. I know—

Lewis: Ralph Kabnis gets satisfied that way?

Kabnis: Satisfied? Say, quit your kiddin. Here, look at that old man there. See him? He's satisfied. Do I look like him? When I'm dead I dont expect t be satisfied. Is that enough f y, with your godam nosin, or do you want more? Well, y wont get it, understand?

Lewis: The old man as symbol, flesh, and spirit of the past, what do think he would say if he could see you? You look at him, Kabnis.

Kabnis: Just like any done-up preacher is what he looks t me. Jam some false teeth in his mouth and crank him, an youd have God Almighty spit in torrents all around th floor. Oh, hell, an he reminds me of that black cockroach over yonder. An besides, he aint my past. My ancestors were Southern blue-bloods—

Lewis: And black.

Kabnis: Aint much difference between blue an black.

Lewis: Enough to draw a denial from you. Cant hold them, can you? Master; slave. Soil; and the overarching heavens. Dusk; dawn. They fight and bastardize you. The sun tint of your cheeks, flame of the great season's multicolored leaves, tarnished, burned. Split, shredded: easily burned. No use . . .

His gaze shifts to Stella. Stella's face draws back, her breasts come towards him.

Stella: I aint got nothin f y, mister. Taint no use t look at me.

Halsey: Youre a queer feller, Lewis, I swear y are. Told y so, didnt I, girls? Just take him easy though, an he'll be ridin just th same as any Georgia mule, eh, Lewis? (Laughs.)

Stella: I'm goin t tell y somethin, mister. It aint t you, t th Mister Lewis what noses about. Its t somethin different, I dunno what. That old man there—maybe its him—is like m father used t look. He used t sing. An when he could sing no mo, they'd allus come f him an carry him t church an there he'd sit, befo th pulpit, aswayin an aleadin every song. A white man took m mother an it broke th old man's heart. He died; an then I didnt care what become of me, an I dont now. I dont care now. Dont get it in y head I'm some sentimental Susie askin for yo sop. Nassur. But theres somethin t yo th others aint got. Boars an kids an fools—thats all I've known. Boars when their fever's up. When their fever's up they come t me. Halsey asks me over when he's off th job. Kabnis—it ud be a sin t play with him. He takes it out in talk.

Halsey knows that he has trifled with her. At odd things

he has been inwardly penitent before her tasking him. But now he wants to hurt her. He turns to Lewis.

Halsey: Lewis, I got a little licker in me, an thats true. True's what I said. True. But th stuff just seems t wake me up an make my mind a man of me. Listen. You know a lot, queer as hell as y arc, an I want t ask y some questions. Theyre too high fer them, Stella an Cora an Kabnis, so we'll just excuse em. A chat between ourselves. (Turns to the others.) You all cant listen in on this. Twont interest y. So just leave th table t this gen'lemun an myself. Go long now.

Kabnis gets up, pompous in his robe, grotesquely so, and makes as if to go through a grand march with Stella. She shoves him off, roughly, and in a mood swings her body to the steps. Kabnis grabs Cora and parades around, passing the old man, to whom he bows in mock-curtsy. He sweeps by the table, snatches the licker bottle, and then he and Cora sprawl on the mattresses. She meets his weak approaches after the manner she thinks Stella would use.

Halsey contemptuously watches them until he is sure that they are settled.

Halsey: This aint th sort o thing f me, Lewis, when I got work upstairs. Nassur. You an me has got things t do. Wastin time on common low-down women—say, Lewis, look at her now—Stella—aint she a picture? Common wench—na she aint, Lewis. You know she aint. I'm only tryin t fool y. I used t love that girl. Yassur. An sometimes when th moon is thick an I hear dogs up th valley barkin an some old woman fetches out her song, an th winds seem like th Lord made them fer t fetch an carry th smell o pine an cane, an there aint no big job on foot, I sometimes get t thinkin that I still do. But I want t talk t y, Lewis, queer as y are. Y know, Lewis, I went t school once. Ya. In Augusta. But it wasnt a regular school. Na. It was a pussy Sunday-school masqueradin under a regular name. Some goody-goody teachers from th North had come down t teach th niggers. If you was nearly white, they liked y. If you was black, they didnt. But it wasnt that—I was all right, y see. I couldnt stand em messin an pawin over m business like I was a child. So I cussed em out an left. Kabnis there ought t have cussed out th old duck over yonder an left. He'd a been a better man tday. But as I was sayin, I couldnt stand their ways. So I left an came here an worked with my father. An been here ever since. He died. I set in f myself. An its always been; give me a good job an sure pay an I aint far from being satisfied, so far as satisfaction goes. Prejudice is everywheres about this country. An a nigger aint in much standin anywheres. But when it comes t pottin round an doin nothing, with nothin bigger'n an ax-handle t hold a feller down, like it was a while back befo I got this job—that beam ought t be—but tmorrow mornin early's time enough f that. As I was sayin, I gets t thinkin. Play dumb naturally t white folks. I gets t thinkin. I used to subscribe t th *Literary Digest*[14] an that helped along a bit. But there werent nothing I could sink m teeth int. Theres lots I want t ask y, Lewis. Been askin y t come around. Couldnt get y. Cant get in much tnight. (He glances at the others. His mind fastens on Kabnis.) Say, tell me this, whats on your mind t say on that feller there? Kabnis' name. One queer bird ought t know another, seems like t me.

Licker has released conflicts in Kabnis and set them flowing. He pricks his ears, intuitively feels that the talk is about him, leaves Cora, and approaches the table. His eyes are watery, heavy with passion. He stoops. He is a ridiculous pathetic figure in his showy robe.

Kabnis: Talkin bout me. I know. I'm th topic of conversation everywhere theres talk about this town. Girls an fellers. White folks as well. An if its me youre talkin bout, guess I got a right t listen in. Whats sayin? Whats sayin bout his royal guts, the Duke? Whats sayin, eh?

Halsey (to Lewis): We'll take it up another time.

Kabnis: No nother time bout it. Now. I'm here now an talkin's just begun. I was born an bred in a family of orators, thats what I was.

Halsey: Preachers.

Kabnis: Na. Preachers hell. I didnt say wind-busters. Y misapprehended me. Y understand what that means, dont y? All right then, y misapprehended me. I didnt say preachers. I said orators. O R A T O R S. Born one an I'll die one. You understand me, Lewis. (He turns to Halsey and begins shaking his finger in his face.) An as f you, youre all right f choppin things from blocks of wood. I was good at that th day I ducked th cradle. An since then, I've been shapin words after a design that branded here. Know whats here? M soul. Ever heard o that? Th hell y have. Been shapin words t fit m soul. Never told y that before, did I? Thought I couldnt talk. I'll tell y. I've been shapin words; ah, but sometimes theyre beautiful an golden an have a taste that makes them fine t roll over with y tongue. Your tongue aint fit f nothin but t roll an lick hog-meat.

Stella and Cora come up to the table.

Halsey: Give him a shove there, will y, Stel?

Stella jams Kabnis in a chair. Kabnis springs up.

Kabnis: Cant keep a good man down. Those words I was tellin y about, they wont fit int th mold thats branded on m soul. Rhyme, y see? Poet, too. Bad rhyme. Bad poet. Somethin else youve learned tnight. Lewis dont know it all, an I'm atellin y. Ugh. Th form thats burned int my soul is some twisted awful thing that crept in from a dream, a godam nightmare, an wont stay still unless I feed it. An it lives on words. Not beautiful words. God Almighty no. Misshapen, split-gut, tortured, twisted words. Layman was feedin it back there that day you thought I ran out fearin things. White folks feed it cause their looks are words. Niggers, black niggers feed it cause theyre evil an their looks are words. Yallar niggers feed it. This whole damn bloated purple country feeds it cause its goin down t hell in a holy avalanche of words. I want t feed th soul—I know what that is; th preachers dont—but I've got t feed it. I wish t God some lynchin white man ud stick his knife through it an pin it to a tree. An pin it to a tree. You hear me? Thats a wish f y, you little snot-nosed pups who've been makin fun of me, an fakin that I'm weak. Me, Ralph Kabnis weak. Ha.

Halsey: Thats right, old man. There, there. Here, so much exertion merits a fittin reward. Help him t be seated, Cora.

Halsey gives him a swig of shine. Cora glides up, seats him, and then plumps herself down on his lap, squeezing his head into her breasts. Kabnis mutters. Tries to break loose. Curses. Cora almost stifles him. He goes limp and gives up. Cora toys with him. Ruffles his hair. Braids it. Parts it in the middle. Stella smiles contemptuously. And then a sudden anger sweeps her. She would like to lash Cora from the place. She'd like to take Kabnis to some distant pine grove and nurse and mother him. Her eyes flash. A quick tensioning throws her breasts and neck into a poised strain. She starts towards them. Halsey grabs her arm and pulls her to him. She struggles. Halsey pins her arms and kisses her. She settles, spurting like a pine-knot afire.

Lewis finds himself completely cut out. The glowing within him subsides. It is followed by a dead chill. Kabnis, Carrie, Stella, Halsey, Cora, the old man, the cellar, and the work-shop, the southern town descend upon him. Their pain is too intense. He cannot stand it. He bolts from the table. Leaps up the stairs. Plunges through the work-shop and out into the night.

6

The cellar swims in a pale phosphorescence. The table, the chairs, the figure of the old man are amœba-like shadows which move about and float in it. In the corner under the steps, close to the floor, a solid blackness. A sound comes from it. A forcible yawn. Part of the blackness detaches itself so that it may be seen against the grayness of the wall. It moves forward and then seems to be clothing itself in odd dangling bits of shadow. The voice of Halsey, vibrant and deepened, calls.

Halsey: Kabnis. Cora. Stella.

He gets no response. He wants to get them up, to get on the job. He is intolerant of their sleepiness.

Halsey: Kabnis! Stella! Cora!

Gutturals, jerky and impeded, tell that he is shaking them.

Halsey: Come now, up with you.

Kabnis (sleepily and still more or less intoxicated): Whats th big idea? What in hell—

Halsey: Work. But never you mind about that. Up with you.

Cora: Oooooo! Look here, mister, I aint used t bein thrown int th street befo day.

Stella: Any bunk whats worked is worth in wages moren this. But come on. Taint no use t arger.

Kabnis: I'll arger. Its preposterous—

The girls interrupt him with none too pleasant laughs.

Kabnis: Thats what I said. Know what it means, dont y? All right, then. I said its preposterous t root an artist out o bed at this ungodly hour, when there aint no use t it. You can start your damned old work. Nobody's stoppin y. But what we got t get up for? Fraid somebody'll see th girls leavin? Some sport, you are. I hand it t y.

Halsey: Up you get, all th same.

Kabnis: Oh, th hell you say.

Halsey: Well, son, seeing that I'm th kindhearted father, I'll give y chance t open your eyes. But up y get when I come down.

He mounts the steps to the work-shop and starts a fire in the hearth. In the yard he finds some chunks of coal which he brings in and throws on the fire. He puts a kettle on to boil. The wagon draws him. He lifts an oak-beam, fingers it, and becomes abstracted. Then comes to himself and places the beam upon the workbench. He looks over some newly cut wooden spokes. He goes to the fire and pokes it. The coals are red-hot. With a pair of long prongs he picks them up and places them in a thick iron bucket. This he carries downstairs. Outside, darkness has given way to the impalpable grayness of dawn. This early morning light, seeping through the four barred cellar windows, is the color of the stony walls. It seems to be an emanation from them. Halsey's coals throw out a rich warm glow. He sets them on the floor, a safe distance from the beds.

Halsey: No foolin now. Come. Up with you.

Other than a soft rustling, there is no sound as the girls slip into their clothes. Kabnis still lies in bed.

Stella (to Halsey): Reckon y could spare us a light?

Halsey strikes a match, lights a cigarette, and then bends over and touches flame to the two candles on the table between the beds. Kabnis asks for a cigarette. Halsey hands him his and takes a fresh one for himself. The girls, before the mirror, are doing up their hair. It is bushy hair that has gone through some straightening process. Character, however, has not all been ironed out. As they kneel there, heavy-eyed and dusky, and throwing grotesque moving shadows on the wall, they are two princesses in Africa going through the early-morning ablutions of their pagan prayers. Finished, they come forward to stretch their hands and warm them over the glowing coals. Red dusk of a Georgia sunset, their heavy, coal-lit faces . . . Kabnis suddenly recalls something.

Kabnis: Th old man talked last night.

Stella: An so did you.

Halsey: In your dreams.

Kabnis: I tell y, he did. I know what I'm talkin about. I'll tell y what he said. Wait now, lemme see.

Halsey: Look out, brother, th old man'll be getting int you by way o dreams. Come, Stel, ready? Cora? Coffee an eggs f both of you.

Halsey goes upstairs.

Stella: Gettin generous, aint he?

She blows the candles out. Says nothing to Kabnis. Then she and Cora follow after Halsey. Kabnis, left to himself, tries to rise. He has slept in his robe. His robe trips him. Finally, he manages to stand up. He starts across the floor. Half-way to the old man, he falls and lies quite still. Perhaps an hour passes. Light of a new sun is about to filter through the windows. Kabnis slowly rises to support upon his elbows. He looks hard, and internally gathers himself together. The side face of Father John is in the direct line of his eyes. He scowls at him. No one is around. Words gush from Kabnis.

Kabnis: You sit there like a black hound spiked to an ivory pedestal. An all night long I heard you murmurin that devil-ish word. They thought I didnt hear y, but I did. Mumblin, feedin that ornery thing thats livin on my insides. Father John. Father of Satan, more likely. What does it mean t you? Youre dead already. Death. What does it mean t you? To you who died way back there in th 'sixties. What are y throwin it in my throat for? Whats it goin t get y? A good smashin in th mouth, thats what. My fist'll sink int y black mush face clear t y guts—if y got any. Dont believe y have. Never seen signs

of none. Death. Death. Sin an Death. All night long y mum-
bled death. (He forgets the old man as his mind begins to
play with the word and its associations.) Death . . . these
clammy floors . . . just like th place they used t stow away th
wornout, no-count niggers in th days of slavery . . . that was
long ago; not so long ago . . . no windows (he rises higher on
his elbows to verify this assertion. He looks around, and,
seeing no one but the old man, calls.) Halsey! Halsey! Gone
an left me. Just like a nigger. I thought he was a nigger all th
time. Now I know it. Ditch y when it comes right down t it.
Damn him anyway. Godam him. (He looks and re-sees the
old man.) Eh, you? T hell with you too. What do I care
whether you can see or hear? You know what hell is cause
youve been there. Its a feelin an its ragin in my soul in a way
that'll pop out of me an run you through, an scorch y, an
burn an rip your soul. Your soul. Ha. Nigger soul. A gin soul
that gets drunk on a preacher's words. An screams. An
shouts. God Almighty, how I hate that shoutin. Where's th
beauty in that? Gives a buzzard a windpipe an I'll bet a dollar t a dime th buzzard ud beat y to it. Aint surprisin th
white folks hate y so. When you had eyes, did you ever see th
beauty of th world? Tell me that. Th hell y did. Now dont tell
me. I know y didnt. You couldnt have. Oh, I'm drunk an just
as good as dead, but no eyes that have seen beauty ever lose
their sight. You aint got no sight. If you had, drunk as I am,
I hope Christ will kill me if I couldnt see it. Your eyes are
dull and watery, like fish eyes. Fish eyes are dead eyes. Youre
an old man, a dead fish man, an black at that. Theyve put y
here t die, damn fool y are not t know it. Do y know how
many feet youre under ground? I'll tell y. Twenty. An do y
think you'll ever see th light of day again, even if you wasnt
blind? Do y think youre out of slavery? Huh? Youre where
they used t throw th worked-out, no-count slaves. On a

damp clammy floor of a dark scum-hole. An they called that an infirmary. Th sons-a . . . . Why I can already see you toppled off that stool an stretched out on th floor beside me— not beside me, damn you, by yourself, with th flies buzzin an lickin God knows what they'd find on a dirty, black, foul-breathed mouth like yours . . .

Some one is coming down the stairs. Carrie, bringing food for the old man. She is lovely in her fresh energy of the morning, in the calm untested confidence and nascent maternity which rise from the purpose of her present mission. She walks to within a few paces of Kabnis.

Carrie K.: Brother says come up now, brother Ralph.

Kabnis: Brother doesnt know what he's talkin bout.

Carrie K.: Yes he does, Ralph. He needs you on th wagon.

Kabnis: He wants me on th wagon, eh? Does he think some wooden thing can lift me up? Ask him that.

Carrie K.: He told me t help y.

Kabnis: An how would you help me, child, dear sweet little sister?

She moves forward as if to aid him.

Carrie K.: I'm not a child, as I've more than once told you, brother Ralph, an as I'll show you now.

Kabnis: Wait, Carrie. No, thats right. Youre not a child. But twont do t lift me bodily. You dont understand. But its th soul of me that needs th risin.

Carrie K.: Youre a bad brother an just wont listen t me when I'm tellin y t go t church.

Kabnis doesnt hear her. He breaks down and talks to himself.

Kabnis: Great God Almighty, a soul like mine cant pin itself onto a wagon wheel an satisfy itself in spinnin round. Iron prongs an hickory sticks, an God knows what all . . . all right for Halsey . . . use him. Me? I get my life down in this scum-hole. Th old man an me—

Carrie K.: Has he been talkin?

Kabnis: Huh? Who? Him? No. Dont need to. I talk. An when I really talk, it pays th best of them t listen. Th old man is a good listener. He's deaf; but he's a good listener. An I can talk t him. Tell him anything.

Carrie K.: He's deaf an blind, but I reckon he hears, an sees too, from th things I've heard.

Kabnis: No. Cant. Cant I tell you. How's he do it?

Carrie K.: Dunno, except I've heard that th souls of old folks have a way of seein things.

Kabnis: An I've heard them call that superstition.

The old man begins to shake his head slowly. Carrie and Kabnis watch him, anxiously. He mumbles. With a grave motion his head nods up and down. And then, on one of the downswings—

Father John (remarkably clear and with great conviction): Sin.

He repeats this word several times, always on the downward nodding. Surprised, indignant, Kabnis forgets that Carrie is with him.

Kabnis: Sin! Shut up. What do you know about sin, you old black bastard. Shut up, an stop that swayin an noddin your head.

Father John: Sin.

Kabnis tries to get up.

Kabnis: Didnt I tell y t shut up?

Carrie steps forward to help him. Kabnis is violently shocked at her touch. He springs back.

Kabnis: Carrie! What . . how . . Baby, you shouldnt be down here. Ralph says things. Doesnt mean to. But Carrie, he doesnt know what he's talkin about. Couldnt know. It was only a preacher's sin they knew in those old days, an that wasnt sin at all. Mind me, th only sin is whats done against th soul. Th whole world is a conspiracy t sin, especially in America, an against me. I'm th victim of their sin. I'm what sin is. Does he look like me? Have you ever heard him say th things youve heard me say? He couldnt if he had th Holy Ghost t help him. Dont look shocked, little sweetheart, you hurt me.

Father John: Sin.

Kabnis: Aw, shut up, old man.

Carrie K.: Leave him be. He wants t say somethin. (She turns to the old man.) What is it, Father?

Kabnis: Whatsha talkin t that old deaf man for? Come away from him.

Carrie K.: What is it, Father?

The old man's lips begin to work. Words are formed incoherently. Finally, he manages to articulate—

Father John: Th sin whats fixed . . . (Hesitates.)

Carrie K. (restraining a comment from Kabnis): Go on, Father.

Father John: . . . upon th white folks—

Kabnis: Suppose youre talkin about that bastard race thats roamin round th country. It looks like sin, if thats what y mean. Give us somethin new an up t date.

Father John :—f tellin Jesus—lies. O th sin th white folks 'mitted when they made th Bible lie.

Boom. Boom. BOOM! Thuds on the floor above. The old man sinks back into his stony silence. Carrie is wet-eyed. Kabnis, contemptuous.

Kabnis: So thats your sin. All these years t tell us that th white folks made th Bible lie. Well, I'll be damned. Lewis ought t have been here. You old black fakir—[15]

Carrie K.: Brother Ralph, is that your best Amen?

She turns him to her and takes his hot cheeks in her firm cool hands. Her palms draw the fever out. With its passing, Kabnis crumples. He sinks to his knees before her, ashamed, exhausted. His eyes squeeze tight. Carrie presses his face tenderly against her. The suffocation of her fresh starched dress feels good to him. Carrie is about to lift her hands in prayer, when Halsey, at the head of the stairs, calls down.

Halsey: Well, well. Whats up? Aint you ever comin? Come on. Whats up down there? Take you all mornin t sleep off a pint? Youre weakenin, man, youre weakenin. Th axle an th beam's all ready waitin f y. Come on.

Kabnis rises and is going doggedly towards the steps. Carrie notices his robe. She catches up to him, points to it, and helps him take it off. He hangs it, with an exaggerated ceremony, on its nail in the corner. He looks down on the tousled beds. His lips curl bitterly. Turning, he stumbles over the bucket of dead coals. He savagely jerks it from the floor. And then, seeing Carrie's eyes upon him, he swings the pail carelessly and with eyes downcast and swollen, trudges upstairs to the work-shop. Carrie's gaze follows him till he is gone. Then she goes to the old man and slips to her knees before him. Her lips murmur, "Jesus, come."

Light streaks through the iron-barred cellar window. Within its soft circle, the figures of Carrie and Father John.

Outside, the sun arises from its cradle in the tree-tops of the forest. Shadows of pines are dreams the sun shakes from its eyes. The sun arises. Gold-glowing child, it steps into the sky and sends a birth-song slanting down gray dust streets and sleepy windows of the southern town.

THE END

Appendix I:
Publication History

The following gives information, in chronological order, on the first publication of pieces brought together in *Cane*, and occasionally on their composition.

1. "Song of the Son," *The Crisis* 23 (April 1922): 261.
2. "Fern," *Little Review* 9 (Autumn 1922): 25–29.
3. "Carma," *The Liberator* 5 (September 1922): 13.
4. "Georgia Dusk," *The Liberator* 5 (September 1922): 25.
5. "Storm Ending," *Double Dealer* 4 (September 1922): 146.
6. "Calling Jesus," *Double Dealer* 4 (September 1922): 132, under the title "Nora."
7. "Becky," *The Liberator* 5 (October 1922): 30.
8. "Seventh Street," *Broom* 4 (December 1922): 3.
9. "Harvest Song," *Double Dealer* 4 (December 1922): 258.
10. "Karintha," *Broom* 4 (January 1922): 83–85. The sketch was included in Toomer's play *Natalie Mann* (unpublished in his lifetime, composed in 1922) as a work written by the prophet of the "new America," Nathan Merilh, a figure clearly based on Toomer's self-conception. In the play, Merilh reads the piece to a background of a hummed folk song; and on the appearance of "Karintha" in *Broom* a note instructs that this is how the piece itself should be read. *Natalie Mann* has now been published in *The Wayward and the Seeking: A*

Collection of Writings by Jean Toomer, ed. Darwin T. Turner (Washington, DC: Howard University Press, 1980).

11. "Face," *Modern Review* 1 (January 1923): 81, appearing as number 2 of "Georgia Portraits."

12. "Portrait in Georgia," *Modern Review* 1 (January 1923): 81, appearing as number 1 of "Georgia Portraits."

13. "Conversion," *Modern Review* 1 (January 1923): 81, appearing as number 3 of "Georgia Portraits." The first five lines formed part of a poem written by the prophet-hero David Teyy in Toomer's short story "Withered Skin of Berries," which was published posthumously in *The Wayward and the Seeking* and written in the summer of 1922, according to a letter to Waldo Frank in July of that year. The poem in "Withered Skin of Berries" reads thus:

> Court-house tower,
> Bell-buoy of the Whites,
> Charting the white-man's channel,
> Bobs on the agitated crests of pines
> And sends its mellow monotone,
> Satirically sweet,
> To guide the drift of barges . . .
> Black barges . . .
>
> African Guardian of Souls,
> Drunk with rum,
> Feasting on a strange cassava,
> Yielding to new words and a weak palabra
> Of a white-faced sardonic god—

14. "Esther," *Modern Review* 1 (January 1923): 50–55.

15. "Blood-Burning Moon," *Prairie* (March–April 1923): 18.

16. "November Cotton Flower," *Nomad* 2 (Summer 1923): 4.

17. "Her Lips Are Copper Wire," *S4N* (May–August 1923).

18. "Kabnis." Toomer originally wrote this piece as a play in December 1921 and hoped it would be produced as such. He revised it into a narrative over a period of a year. Section one first appeared in *Broom* 5 (August 1923): 12–16; sections five and six appeared in the September issue of the same journal.

Appendix II:
1923 Foreword by Waldo Frank

Reading this book, I had the vision of a land, heretofore sunk in the mists of muteness, suddenly rising up into the eminence of song. Innumerable books have been written about the South; some good books have been written in the South. This book *is* the South. I do not mean that *Cane* covers the South or is the South's full voice. Merely this: a poet has arisen among our American youth who has known how to turn the essences and materials of his Southland into the essences and materials of literature. A poet has arisen in that land who writes, not as a Southerner, not as a rebel against Southerners, not as a Negro, not as apologist or priest or critic: who writes as a *poet*. The fashioning of beauty is ever foremost in his inspiration: not forcedly but simply, and because these ultimate aspects of his world are to him more real than all its specific problems. He has made songs and lovely stories of his land . . . not of its yesterday, but of its immediate life. And that has been enough.

How rare this is will be clear to those who have followed with concern the struggle of the South toward literary expression, and the particular trial of that portion of its folk whose skin is dark. The gifted Negro has been too often

thwarted from becoming a poet because his world was forever forcing him to recollect that he was a Negro. The artist
must lose such lesser identities in the great well of life. The
English poet is not forever protesting and recalling that he is
English. It is so natural and easy for him to be English that
he can sing as a man. The French novelist is not forever not-
ing: "This is French." It is so atmospheric for him to be
French, that he can devote himself to saying: "This is
human." This is an imperative condition for the creating of
deep art. The whole will and mind of the creator must go
below the surfaces of race. And this has been an almost impossible condition for the American Negro to achieve, forced
every moment of his life into a specific and superficial plane
of consciousness.

The first negative significance of *Cane* is that this so natural
and restrictive state of mind is completely lacking. For Toomer,
the Southland is not a problem to be solved; it is a field of loveliness to be sung: the Georgia Negro is not a downtrodden
soul to be uplifted; he is material for gorgeous painting: the
segregated self-conscious brown belt of Washington is not a
topic to be discussed and exposed; it is a subject of beauty and
of drama, worthy of creation in literary form.

It seems to me, therefore, that this is a first book in more
ways than one. It is a harbinger of the South's literary maturity: of its emergence from the obsession put upon its minds by
the unending racial crisis—an obsession from which writers
have made their indirect escape through sentimentalism,
exoticism, polemic, "problem" fiction, and moral melodrama.
It marks the dawn of direct and unafraid creation. And, as the
initial work of a man of twenty-seven, it is the harbinger of a
literary force of whose incalculable future I believe no reader
of this book will be in doubt.

How typical is *Cane* of the South's still virgin soil and of its pressing seeds! and the book's chaos of verse, tale, drama, its rhythmic rolling shift from lyrism to narrative, from mystery to intimate pathos! But read the book through and you will see a complex and significant form take substance from its chaos. Part One is the primitive and evanescent black world of Georgia. Part Two is the threshing and suffering brown world of Washington, lifted by opportunity and contact into the anguish of self-conscious struggle. Part Three is Georgia again . . . the invasion into this black womb of the ferment seed: the neurotic, educated, spiritually stirring Negro. As a broad form this is superb, and the very looseness and unexpected waves of the book's parts make *Cane* still more *South*, still more of an aesthetic equivalent of the land.

What a land it is! What an Aeschylean beauty to its fateful problem! Those of you who love our South will find here some of your love. Those of you who know it not will perhaps begin to understand what a warm splendor is at last at dawn.

> A feast of moon and men and barking hounds,
> An orgy for some genius of the South
> With bloodshot eyes and cane-lipped scented mouth
> Surprised in making folk-songs . . . .

So, in his still sometimes clumsy stride (for Toomer is finally a poet in prose) the author gives you an inkling of his revelation. An individual force, wise enough to drink humbly at this great spring of his land . . . such is the first impression of Jean Toomer. But beyond this wisdom and this power (which shows itself perhaps most splendidly in his complete freedom from the sense of persecution), there rises a figure more significant: the artist, hard, self-immolating, the artist who is not interested in races, whose domain is Life. The book's final Part is no longer "promise"; it is achievement. It is no mere dawn: it is a bit of the full morning. These materials . . . the ancient black man, mute, inaccessible, and yet so mystically close to the new tumultuous members of his race, the simple slave Past, the shredding Negro Present, the iridescent passionate dream of the To-morrow . . . are made and measured by a craftsman into an unforgettable music. The notes of his counterpoint are particular, the themes are of intimate connection with us Americans. But the result is that abstract and absolute thing called Art.

WALDO FRANK

Notes

FOREWORD

1. Rudolph P. Byrd and Henry Louis Gates Jr., "'Song of the Son': The Emergence and Passing of Jean Toomer," in *Cane: Authoritative Text, Contexts, Criticism*, 2nd ed. (New York: Norton, 2011).

INTRODUCTION

1. Montgomery Gregory, "Our Book Shelf," *Opportunity* 1 (1923): 374.
2. Waldo Frank, foreword to *Cane*, Jean Toomer (New York: Boni & Liveright, 1923), ix.
3. Except where noted otherwise, I have relied for biographical information on Cynthia Earl Kerman and Richard Eldridge, *The Lives of Jean Toomer: A Hunger for Wholeness* (Westport, CT: Avi, 1970), 416–33.
4. Quoted in Kerman and Eldridge, *The Lives of Jean Toomer*, 66.
5. Toomer to Liveright, March 9, 1923, in *The Letters of Jean Toomer, 1919–1924*, ed. Mark Whalan (Knoxville: University of Tennessee Press, 2006), 137.
6. Waldo Frank, *Our America* (New York: Boni & Liveright, 1919).
7. W. E. B. DuBois, *The Souls of Black Folk* (1903; reprint New York: Penguin, 1989), 11–12.

8. Alain Locke, foreword to *The New Negro*, ed. Alain Locke (1925; reprint New York: Atheneum, 1992), xxv–xxvi.

9. Jean Toomer to Mae Wright, August 4, 1922, in *Letters*, 62.

10. Jean Toomer to *The Liberator*, August 19, 1922, in *Letters*, 70–71.

11. Jean Toomer to Sherwood Anderson, December 29, 1922, in *Letters*, 106.

12. Jean Toomer to Gorham Munson, October 31, 1922, in *Letters*, 90–91.

13. Jean Toomer, "The Critic of Waldo Frank: Criticism, an Art Form," in *Jean Toomer: Selected Essays and Literary Criticism*, ed. Robert B. Jones (Knoxville: University of Tennessee Press, 1996), 28, 29.

14. Jean Toomer to Waldo Frank, December 12, 1922, in *Letters*, 101.

15. Jean Toomer to Horace Liveright, September 5, 1923, in *Letters*, 171.

16. Jean Toomer to Claude Barnett, April 29, 1923, in *Letters*, 159–60.

17. Toomer to Liveright, September 5, 1923, in *Letters*, 171.

18. Aaron Douglas to Alta Sawyer, [1925], Aaron Douglas Papers, Schomburg Center for Research in Black Culture, New York Public Library. Quoted in George Hutchinson, *In Search of Nella Larsen: A Biography of the Color Line* (Cambridge, MA: Harvard University Press, 2006), 185.

19. Jean Toomer, "The Negro Emergent," in *Jean Toomer: Selected Essays*, 54.

20. "Reception to Jean Toomer," *New York Age*, May 2, 1925, p. 2; "Library Notes," *Amsterdam News*, April 15, 1925, p. 7; "135th Street Library News," *Amsterdam News*, April 29, 1925, p. 14; John Farrar, "The Gossip Shop," *Bookman* 61 (1925): 624.

21. Jean Toomer, "On Being an American," typescript, p. 52, Jean Toomer Papers, Beinecke Rare Book and Manuscript Library, Yale University.

22. Toomer's draft registration cards for both world wars, for example, identify him as "Negro," whereas one of his marriage licenses identifies him as "white." Rudolph P. Byrd and Henry

Louis Gates Jr. have tried to wrestle this into an argument that Toomer was a black man passing as white, in their introduction to Jean Toomer, *Cane*, ed. Byrd and Gates (New York: W. W. Norton, 2011), lxx.

23. Allyson Hobbs, *A Chosen Exile: A History of Racial Passing in American Life* (Cambridge, MA: Harvard University Press, 2014), p. 194

EPIGRAPH

1. *Redolent of fermenting syrup . . . / Deep-rooted cane*: The cane, or stalk, of sweet sorghum produces a sweet juice when crushed in a mill, which is then boiled into a syrup, the source of molasses. The syrup was often used instead of sugar in the mash of cornmeal, yeast, water, and malt that was fermented to produce corn whiskey, or moonshine. Also significant is the fact that sorghum seeds were first carried to the New World in the seventeenth and eighteenth centuries by captives from Africa, where the plant had been cultivated for many centuries.

KARINTHA

1. *stills*: A moonshine still was an apparatus for illegally distilling whiskey, common in the rural South during the years of Prohibition, and a significant source of cash for poor farmers.

NOVEMBER COTTON FLOWER

1. *Boll-weevil's coming*: The cotton boll weevil is an insect that attacks the boll of the cotton plant, depositing eggs in the cotton square, which then shrivels and falls to the ground with the larvae inside. By 1922, 90 percent of the cotton belt was overrun by the boll weevil. Severe infestations in Georgia in the early 1920s drove many tenant farmers out of the region.

BECKY

1. *a hant*: A ghost.

CARMA

1. *Carma*: Toomer apparently wants to suggest the Hindu and Buddhist concept of karma, according to which all of one's actions in a given state of existence determine the nature of one's next life.
2. *guinea's squawk*: referring to the sound of a guinea hen, a domesticated fowl common in West Africa as well as the American South.
3. *mazda*: According to the Zend-Avesta, a sacred text of ancient Persia, Ahura Mazda was the creator of the world, associated with the light-giving heavens. In the early twentieth century, General Electric adopted the term as the trademark for a high-quality lightbulb.
4. *juju men, greegree*: Juju is a colloquial term for conjuring practices derived from Africa. Greegree, or "gris-gris" in the more common French spelling, refers to an amulet or charm thought to have powers of protection, healing, or destruction.
5. *Her husband's in the gang*: A chain gang, particularly common in the South, is a group of chained prisoners put to work on road repair and other hard labor for the state, or contracted out to private enterprises.
6. *canebrake*: A dense thicket of cane.

GEORGIA DUSK

1. *vesper*: evening prayer service.

FERN

1. *Jewish cantor*: Singer of solo religious chants in a synagogue.
2. *a prostitute along State Street in Chicago*: In the 1910s and 1920s, State Street in the Near South Side of Chicago was a

notorious area of saloons, gambling, and prostitution, more or less tolerated by the police because the population of the area was mainly black and poor.

3. *the Pullman or the Jim Crow*: A Pullman car had private sleeping compartments. Blacks were generally barred from such cars in the segregated South and forced to travel in the black-only "Jim Crow" cars, which were often uncomfortable and badly maintained.

NULLO

1. *Nullo*: "A nought, a cipher," signifying nothing in itself but increasing or decreasing the value of other figures according to its position (*Oxford English Dictionary*).

ESTHER

1. *five fingers full of shine*: The soda bottles are filled with moonshine whiskey up to the width of five fingers.
2. *Indian fakir*: A Hindu ascetic, or Islamic religious mendicant, often claiming the ability to perform miracles.
3. *Cut-out open*: A stylish sedan with an open top.
4. *dictie niggers*: A pejorative term for relatively well-off African Americans, especially those suspected of setting themselves above other black people.

BLOOD-BURNING MOON

1. *Blood-burning moon*: Revelation 6.12 in the Bible refers to John of Patmos's vision of a night when "the moon became as blood," foretelling Jesus's second coming, when he would save the righteous and destroy the wicked. This became the basis of a folk belief that a red moon is an omen of violence.
2. *pre-war cotton factory*: A textile factory, based on an actual abandoned factory building on the outskirts of Sparta, Georgia (Foley, "Jean Toomer's Sparta").

3. *factory town*: A location of antebellum cotton mills.
4. *craps*: A game of dice that involves gambling.
5. *on th gang*: On the chain gang. See note 5 in the chapter titled "Carma."

SEVENTH STREET

1. *Seventh Street*: A street in the heart of the black community of Washington, D.C., largely poor and working-class, and the main stopping point for black migrants from the South.
2. *Bootleggers*: People who sold or transported whiskey illegally. The term originally applied to men who hid liquor in the legs of their boots for illicit sale to Indians.
3. *Prohibition*: Following the passage of the Eighteenth Amendment to the Constitution, outlawing the sale of alcohol, the Prohibition period lasted from 1920 to 1933.

RHOBERT

1. *"Deep River"*: A famous African American spiritual. Its opening and closing verses are "Deep river, my home is over Jordan, / Deep river, Lord; I want to cross over into camp ground."

AVEY

1. *V Street*: In northwest Washington, D.C., a mostly black, middle-class neighborhood at the time.
2. *Harpers Ferry*: The location of Storer College, a black school and a popular resort for well-heeled African Americans, including Toomer's family, in the early twentieth century. Harpers Ferry was made famous in 1859 by the raid John Brown led on the federal armory there, hoping to set off a slave revolt. Brown was captured and hanged, becoming a martyr to the abolitionist cause and a seeming prophet of the coming war.

3. *normal school*: A school between high school and college, and the normal preparation for teaching primary and secondary grades at the time.

4. *U Street*: In northwest Washington, D.C., this street became a rather fashionable address for African Americans during the mid-teens. It was also a thoroughfare of black business and entertainment. Jean Toomer lived with his grandparents in an apartment on U Street from 1912 into the early 1920s, including the period in which he composed and published *Cane*.

5. *Soldier's Home*: Located on the northwest outskirts of Washington, D.C., the Soldiers' Home was originally a home for aging war veterans, set on 500 acres of park land. Just to the south was Howard University, and to the north the famous Rock Creek Cemetery.

6. *Howard Glee Club*: A renowned singing club at Howard University.

7. *"Deep River"*: See note 1 in the chapter titled "Rhobert."

THEATER

1. *near-beer saloons*: Saloons selling nonalcoholic beer.

2. *Howard Theater*: Under African American management, this theater served as a kind of community cultural center for black Washington in the early twentieth century. Located at Seventh and T streets, it staged musical hits, plays, and burlesque and minstrel shows, and could be rented for amateur performances. It introduced to black Washington many entertainers who went on to become Broadway stars. Jean Toomer worked as assistant to the manager for two weeks in the fall of 1922.

3. *Put . . . and take*: A dance move.

4. *Her hair . . . is bobbed*: Bobbed hair was a popular short hairstyle for young women in the 1920s, associated with a new sexual freedom and rebellion against conventional standards of femininity.

5. *stage-door johnny*: A young man who hangs around theaters to meet actresses and chorus girls.

6. *Dictie*: See note 4 in the chapter titled "Esther."

7. *shimmy*: A quick undulating movement of the lower torso.

8. *Chicken Chaser*: A dance number.

9. *Professor*: A colloquial African American term for a piano player, usually in a jazz band.

BOX SEAT

1. *Box seat*: The most expensive seats in the theater, above stage level, usually enclosed by curtains on three sides for privacy.

2. *wool-blossoms*: Referring to tightly curled, so-called "woolly" hair. The "dreaming nigger" that is the street, the narrator suggests, has what many people of the time would consider "pure" Negro features.

3. *liver lips*: A pejorative epithet for large, thick, dark lips.

4. *Thirteenth Street*: A street in Washington, D.C., extending to the northwest. Toomer no doubt has in mind the section where it crosses U and V streets, with mostly black middle-class residents at the time.

5. *Jack the Ripper*: Unknown criminal who murdered and mutilated six prostitutes in London's East End between August and November 1888.

6. *street car*: Streetcars run on rails in the middle of the street; they were the chief means of urban transportation in the early to mid-twentieth century.

7. *the Lincoln*: Lincoln Theatre, located on U Street between Twelfth and Thirteenth streets, opened in February 1922 under black management and seated 1,600.

8. *whishadwash*: Toomer attempts to convey the sound of the crowd coming into the theater and finding their seats.

9. *crimson box-draperies*: The drapery framing the front of the box seats and closing behind them.

10. *bobbed hair*: See note 4 in the chapter titled "Theater."

11. *where was Moses when the light went out?*: A popular trick question. Answer: "In the dark!"

12. *Suppose Gabriel should blow his trumpet!*: According to Christian belief, the archangel Gabriel, who announced the

future birth of John the Baptist to Zacharias and appeared to the Virgin Mary, will blow his trumpet on Judgment Day.

13. *Too much powder*: Referring to "skin-lightening" powder, used by some black women at the time to make their skin color appear more nearly white.

14. *Ery*: This may be a typographical error for "ergo"—a Latin term, rather formal and pedantic to American ears, signifying "therefore" or "it follows that," to mark the conclusion of a syllogism in formal logic.

15. *Swing low, sweet chariot. . . . LET MY PEOPLE GO!*: Dan mentally combines phrases and images from several black spirituals such as "Swing Low, Sweet Chariot," "Roll, Jordan, Roll," and "Go Down, Moses."

16. *the first horse-cars*: Public transportation predating the electric streetcars, when horses pulled the cars.

17. *Walt Whitman*: The celebrated nineteenth-century "poet of democracy," Whitman had lived in Washington from late 1862 to 1873. In the 1920s his work was associated with cultural and social radicalism; Toomer regarded him as a great New World prophet.

18. *a dynamo*: An electric generator.

BONA AND PAUL

1. *bloomers*: Loose pants gathered at the knee, worn by women as part of a gym or sports outfit.

2. *the men*: Possibly a typographical error for "the man."

3. *the South-Side L track*: The elevated railroad that runs south from the center of Chicago, which became a dividing line in the early 1900s between white and black neighborhoods in the Near South Side.

4. *Loop-jammed L trains*: Trains crowded with passengers from the Loop, Chicago's central business district.

5. *the stock-yards*: Area of Chicago's slaughterhouses and meat-packing industries, located in the South Side a few blocks west of the L. The animals were unloaded from trains and held in large pens until they were slaughtered.

6. *The picture of Our Poets*: Schoolrooms and homes of the late nineteenth and early twentieth centuries often featured a row of portraits (captioned "Our Poets") of beloved American poets such as Bryant, Longfellow, Whittier, and Holmes, who were considered genteel Victorians by the 1920s.

7. *a large Negro . . . who guards the door*: As Barbara Foley points out in "Jean Toomer's Washington," it is not unlikely that one job of the black door guard is to keep other blacks from entering the nightclub. The South Side of Chicago, where the club is located, witnessed intense struggles over racial integration, especially after 1915. Many whites were violently antagonistic to interracial socializing and dancing, which raised the specter of interracial sex and black men marrying white women.

8. *Liza, Little Liza Jane*: A popular song, originally from a successful black musical.

9. *a priori*: A Latin term meaning "by prior assumption," reasoning from abstract notions to their conditions or consequences, from propositions or assumed axioms rather than from experience.

KABNIS

1. *Waldo Frank*: A famous (white) American author at the time with whom Toomer developed an intense intellectual comradeship during the composition of *Cane*. Both men thought of *Cane* and Frank's novel *Holiday* as companion texts about the South.

2. *In Camp Ground*: Literally, a place of rest during a journey or the place of an evangelical "camp-meeting" revival; metaphorically, heaven. Toomer is drawing once again from the imagery and symbolism of the spiritual "Deep River": "My home is over Jordan / . . . I want to cross over into camp ground." In a letter to Waldo Frank written while he was completing *Cane*, Toomer wrote that these verses suggested the southern black folk life was going to die or be "absorbed" into a new, modern American identity. See also note 1 in the chapter titled "Rhobert."

3. *rock a-by baby*: Traditional English lullaby. The first, third, fifth, and seventh lines of Toomer's poem come from the lullaby, with which he has intertwined the narrative of a black mother nursing a white infant. Black women often served as wet nurses for white families in the South.

4. *Old Chromo*: A slang term for an obnoxious person.

5. *the Mason and Dixie line*: The Mason-Dixon Line, named for the men who surveyed it in the late 1760s, divided Pennsylvania from Maryland and came to signify the boundary between North and South.

6. *that stir about those peonage cases*: Peonage is the holding of people in servitude to pay off debts or to serve a penal sentence. In a famous peonage and murder case in early 1921, a white Georgia planter, John S. Williams, was convicted of the brutal murder of several black farmworkers. Federal agents had visited the farm to investigate rumors of peonage there, and to avoid conviction the planter had the men killed. Reported throughout the United States, the trial marked the first time in the history of Georgia that a white man was found guilty of killing a man of color, and largely on the testimony of an African American.

7. *th Amen corner*: Usually to the side of the pulpit in some Protestant churches, where leaders of the congregation's responsive "amens" sit.

8. *The story of Mame Lamkins*: Based on an actual incident in which a pregnant black woman was murdered, her abdomen cut open, and the fetus run through with a knife.

9. *My Lord, what a mourning, / When the stars begin to fall*: Lines from a popular spiritual about the last days before the end of the world. Other important verses include: "You'll hear the trumpets sound / To wake the nations underground."

10. *Shinin is th only business what pays in these hard times*: Distilling and selling moonshine whiskey is the only way of gaining cash. Corn liquor, distilled from a mash of fermented cornmeal, sugar or molasses, water, yeast, and malt, was indeed a major cash crop in the southern highlands. A bushel of corn would bring many times the amount of money in the form of whiskey that it would bring as grain, and the whiskey was more easily transported.

11. *Vulcan*: Ancient Roman god of fire and metalworking, Vulcan was originally associated with lightning, and later with volcanoes. His forge was under Mount Etna. Also associated by Christians with the Old Testament figure Tubal-Cain, the son of Lamech and Zillah who invented the art of forging metals.

12. *John the Baptist*: The Jewish prophet who, according to the New Testament, foretold the coming of a messiah and baptized Jesus.

13. *Done up in shine*: Drunk on moonshine.

14. *Literary Digest*: A mass-circulation magazine, founded in 1890, that digested articles from contemporary periodicals. In the early 1920s it had over a million subscribers.

15. *fakir*: See note 2 in the chapter titled "Esther."

Ready to find
your next great classic?

Let us help.

Visit prh.com/penguinclassics